Mrs. Pollifax
and
the
Whirling Dervish

Mrs. Pollifax and

Doubleday

NEW YORK LONDON TORONTO SYDNEY AUCKLAND

the
Whirling Dervish

Dorothy Gilman

PUBLISHED BY DOUBLEDAY
a division of Bantam Doubleday Dell Publishing Group, Inc.
666 Fifth Avenue, New York, New York 10103

DOUBLEDAY and the portrayal of an anchor
with a dolphin are trademarks of Doubleday,
a division of Bantam Doubleday Dell
Publishing Group, Inc.

Library of Congress Cataloging-in-Publication Data

Gilman, Dorothy, 1923–
Mrs. Pollifax and the whirling dervish / Dorothy Gilman. — 1st ed.
p. cm.
I. Title.
PS3557.I433M69   1990
813'.54—dc20   89-25796
                                                                                CIP

ISBN 0-385-41458-7

FIRST EDITION

BVG

to Howard Morhaim

with admiration,
affection, and
many thanks

Mrs. Pollifax
and
the
Whirling Dervish

Prologue

They had been waiting among the low dunes for two days, a few goats feeding nearby on an impoverished growth of desert grass. They were Reguibat, members of a tribe that had made the Sahara their home for centuries, and they gave every evidence of being no more than pastoral nomads except that each man wore a nine-millimeter submachine gun strapped to his back and the tents behind them concealed a pair of camouflaged Land Rovers. They wore coarse khaki-colored *djellabahs* that melted into the khaki-brown of the desert around them and their heads were snugly wrapped in turbans that hid their chins and all but their eyes. In the flat empty expanse of desert nothing moved except a vulture that drifted down from the sky to look over the small *frig,* or encampment, curious as to whether the two men lying across the slight rise in the ground were dead or alive, and then—as one of the men lifted binoculars to his eyes—the vulture, cheated, wheeled and flew on, heading south.

The older man said, "He should have been here yesterday and I do not think he comes to us today, either."

His companion nodded. "It is not good. We go at sunset?"

The older man grunted. "Already we've stayed too long, it's fortunate for us no planes have seen us, only the vultures." With a glance at the sun he nodded. "One more hour and we load tents and goats and leave."

3

"You think there's been trouble? His message spoke of danger, he felt himself watched."

The older man had not exhausted his faith. "His message said also that if not this week he will be with us next week." He nodded. "Insh'Allah, he will come." He adjusted his binoculars to look again yet still there was nothing to be seen but empty desert and a horizon that shifted and shimmered under the merciless sun, and presently they returned to their tents to wait for darkness.

I. *Carstairs* sat at his desk high in the CIA building and studied the photograph that lay in front of him. "I don't like him, Bishop," he said crossly. "I don't like at *all* the choice they made for us in Cairo, I feel damn uneasy sending this man into Morocco alone. It's too important a job—there are seven lives at stake, damn it!"

His assistant, seated across the desk from him, said politely, "Cairo's always been reliable in the past, sir, is there some specific reason for all these 'damns'? I admit that Janko's moustache is rather too ornate for my taste, but otherwise—"

Carstairs was scowling. "You're overlooking his face, Bishop, the eyes, the mouth. He looks brash for a Moslem country, he looks *arrogant*. I realize he's the only person available at short notice who speaks Arabic but still—" His voice faded as his scowl deepened. "You know how vulnerable the Atlas group is, just one slip, one rash decision, one wrong person—" He shook his head. "Suddenly after years of enmity Morocco and Algeria are establishing diplomatic relations and who knows what will happen, what nooses may tighten or—if

5

you'll excuse the mix of metaphors—what hells could break loose for our Atlas group, especially if we're exposed. And now *this*."

Patiently Bishop tried again. "It could be a very poor photo, you know. A pity he's in Cairo and you can't see him or you might feel differently. I don't quite understand what's on your mind, sir."

"I don't either," growled Carstairs, "but it's a very clear photograph and this man Janko doesn't feel right to me. I realize we're stuck and there's no one else to send but I'd feel a hell of a lot better—given the look of him—if he could travel *with* someone, someone to keep an eye on him, to round out his image of tourist—he just doesn't look like a casual tourist. Someone who could dilute his personality, which strikes me as superior and abrasive, someone to keep him—"

"Non-brash?"

"My dear Bishop . . . !"

"Sorry," Bishop said meekly.

Carstairs grinned. "All right, I admit I'm being woefully inarticulate but I can tell you what he needs: a Mrs. Pollifax."

At once Bishop understood, and was awed by Carstairs' cleverness. Carstairs tended to see things in pictures, and at mention of Mrs. Pollifax an unholy glee filled Bishop at such creativeness: he looked again at the photo on the desk, at the fierce black eyebrows, thick black moustache and haughty countenance of the man Janko, and he placed it in the company of cheerful, friendly Mrs. Pollifax—so innocent and trustworthy on sight—and he laughed. "I see what you mean *precisely*," he said. "Especially about the diluting. Emily would be a great leavening influence and she could patch up any PR gaffs that might get him into trouble."

Carstairs nodded. "This Max Janko may be a whiz at languages—apparently that's his specialty—but I doubt from the look of him if he has the slightest idea what the word tact means." His smile faded. "Unfortunately there's only one Emily Pollifax and we can scarcely ask Cyrus to lend us his wife to travel with another man."

A smile grew slowly on Bishop's face and very casually, with a touch of mischief, he said, "I happen to know that Cyrus left three days ago to see his new grandson in Kenya, which happens to be where his daughter and her doctor-husband live now . . ."

Carstairs stared at him. "Alone? Mrs. Pollifax didn't go with him?"

Bishop's smile broadened. "No sir."

"Why?" asked Carstairs. "Nothing wrong between them, I hope."

"As I understand it," said Bishop, "there has been a recent infusion of new grandchildren and they've decided to divide their responsibilities to the next generation before it exhausts them both. He'll be away for two weeks."

"Hmmmm," murmured Carstairs thoughtfully. "Leaving Mrs. Pollifax to tend her geraniums, I suppose." He was silent for a moment and then he nodded and snapped his fingers. "Let's go for it, Bishop, except—" He hesitated, frowning. He still found it ironic that an experimental group set up in '76 as a "checks and balances" experiment had continued unnoticed and unmolested all these years. It seemed a supreme example of unwieldy bureaucracy that once something was begun it developed a weight and a momentum of its own and was rendered invisible: it existed, therefore it *was* . . . He utterly believed in the Atlas group but it continued to amuse him that in this case the right hand didn't know what the left hand was doing, even at Central Intelligence. He said, "I wonder how much she ought to be told? Do we tell her she'll be working for a maverick group, quite secret, called Atlas, and not, officially speaking, for the main arm of the CIA?"

Bishop said with a smile, "I think she might be relieved to hear that, sir. I had a very irate letter from her during the Iran-Contra hearings with innumerable quotes from the U.S. Constitution."

Carstairs smiled faintly. "Nevertheless we can't afford to let her know too much, it would be dangerous."

"It could protect her as well," pointed out Bishop.

Carstairs was silent, considering; reaching his decision he said crisply, "I don't think so. Basically this is a very simple reconnaissance trip. The greatest danger is that of exposure but since there are to be no personal contacts made during the trip there's small likelihood of that—*so long as this Janko chap behaves himself,*" he added tartly. "If Mrs. Pollifax can go, if she's available, it can be emphasized that she's working for a separate department, but anything more than that—" He shook his head.

Bishop said lightly, "On the theory that she may not currently trust the CIA but she trusts us?"

Carstairs smiled. "Our hands are clean—well, relatively speaking," he said dryly. "See if you can reach her by phone, Bishop, and ask if she can possibly leave on tomorrow's flight to Morocco to do a job for us, and if so—God help us if she can't—you'll knock on her door this afternoon and brief her."

"Delighted," said Bishop happily, "and if you'll excuse me now I'll race with appropriate haste to my phone, with fingers crossed all the way."

"A small prayer might help, too," Carstairs called after him but Bishop had already vanished into his office, the door slamming behind him.

Mrs. Pollifax had begun her morning by cutting back a few of the geraniums in her new greenhouse but after clipping three of them she had found herself staring moodily out of the window. *I haven't the slightest interest in doing this,* she thought, and putting aside her garden shears she walked into the kitchen, poured herself a cup of coffee and carried it to the dining table where she did her best thinking.

Something was wrong, she admitted, and she began to cautiously approach what it might be. She could find no regrets that she'd not flown to Kenya with Cyrus; after all, they had spent Christmas with her son Roger in Chicago, and New Year's with her daughter Jane in Arizona, and it had been very pleasant to return home, except that neither of them had expected Lisa's baby to arrive a month early and the news to reach them before they'd even unpacked their bags from Christmas.

Perhaps too many guest rooms had tired her, she thought, or perhaps it was simply the fact that it was January, and the skies unendingly gray, but neither thought produced any response, and impatiently she discarded both. Probing deeper she brought up a discovery that shocked her: she was bored—horribly, depletingly and dispiritingly bored.

Oh God, she thought, *bored?*

And at once she knew—as a part of her had known all along—what was missing in her life. *It's been a whole year,* she thought, *have they decided I'm too old?*

"They," she said aloud, crossly, refusing to name Carstairs, Bishop and the Department, and she gazed unseeingly out of the window at the garden that a January thaw had turned into mud.

It was some years now since Mrs. Pollifax, bored and lonely, had made a daring trip to the CIA to confide her childhood dream of becoming a spy and to volunteer her services. By purest chance—but it had been a miracle, surely?—

she had been noticed in the waiting room by Carstairs, who was in desperate need of an Innocent Tourist for an important courier job, and off she had gone to Mexico. Since then it seemed to her as if her real life had been lived on those occasions when she abandoned committees and Garden Club to go out into the world on assignments for him. After all, this was how she'd met Cyrus, as well as an assortment of other fascinating people, a few of them bent on killing her, but none of whom she would ever have met at her Garden Club.

I'm spoiled, she thought, *I've grown accustomed to those interruptions in my life that send the adrenaline racing and the fight-or-flight responses into high gear, and I cannot—simply cannot—experience either of these with my geraniums, or the Garden Club, and Cyrus is wonderful but I suspect that after last January's adventure, and our nearly being killed in the highlands of Thailand, he is very happy to live quietly and to still be alive.*

As am I, she added quickly and contritely, yet so—so unchallenged that even her weekly karate lessons had begun to seem without point, and giving the knife its final twist she said aloud, "And just maybe you really *are* too old now for adventuring, Emily Pollifax."

The phone's ringing startled her but did not in any way lighten her dark and brooding thoughts. She knew—absolutely *knew*—that it would be either Amos calling from Green Acres Supply House to report the arrival of her fertilizer, or Mrs. Tilliwit to remind her of the Save-Our-Environment meeting on Wednesday. Reluctantly she abandoned her coffee and stilled the phone on its fifth ring.

"Hello," she said, and sighed.

"What a greeting," said a sympathetic and very familiar voice. "I hope I'm not interrupting a wake?"

"B-Bishop?" she faltered. *"Bishop?"*

"None other," he assured her. "Anything wrong?"

She laughed shakily. "Only an excruciating attack of January boredom."

"What an appropriate moment then," he said cheerfully, "to ask if you could possibly leave on tomorrow's flight to Morocco, on an errand strictly for Carstairs. For about a week, in which case—"

"Morocco," she gasped, and at once knew the luxury of anticipation again, and of being useful, felt the walls of her life expand and her sense of claustrophobia dissolve. *Not* too old, she thought, singing the words to herself, *not too old, not too old* . . . and very simply she said, "Yes, Bishop, I can fly to Morocco tomorrow night, I'd be delighted."

"Wonderful! I'll be with you by mid-afternoon to tell you all about it. Check your passport—no visas or vaccinations necessary—and start packing."

He hung up and when she put down the phone she was astonished to see that the living room in which she stood had come to life, too, its colors brilliant against white walls, the solitary geranium on the table a flaming red. And yet how drab it had all looked a few minutes ago, she thought, it wasn't the room, it was *me*, and I allowed it. She added crossly, "Yes, and now that I've said yes to Morocco I suppose I'll suddenly remember all the hazards involved in Carstairs' assignments and be appalled by my recklessness."

She laughed aloud. How difficult it was to be a human being, and how difficult to be consistent. She comforted herself by remembering that Emerson had called consistency the hobgoblin of small minds, and having thus scolded and consoled herself she walked happily upstairs to pack two carry-on bags and wait for Bishop.

He arrived at half-past two. The coffee was beginning to bubble indignantly when she heard the sound of a car sweeping up the graveled driveway and hurried to the door to open it for him. It had been months since she'd seen him, and as he climbed out of a bright red car she greeted him with a joyous, "Bishop —a Jaguar?"

"Strictly rental," he said, grinning at her as he pulled his ubiquitous briefcase from the front seat. "When I was eighteen it was a jeep, in my twenties and thirties it didn't matter, but when one begins losing the vestiges of youth one turns to this sort of toy."

"It happens," she said, nodding. "But what prompted this choice bit of profoundness?"

"Middle age," he said, walking up the steps and adding gloomily, "I shall turn forty in two months."

"Shocking," she told him. "Come in and drown your midlife crisis in coffee and tell me about Morocco."

"Good," he said and tossed his coat over the arm of a chair. "Let's talk in the kitchen, I like kitchens. Bachelors rarely see kitchens and I *like* them."

"And I never knew," she said dryly. "One of those unguessed dimensions about you, Bishop!"

Heading into the cheerfully bright kitchen he placed his briefcase on the table and sat down, smiling happily at her. "I'm filled with dimensions that people fail to notice, it's the despair of my life."

"Especially the blondes you dote on?"

"Especially the blondes."

"I refuse to feel sorry for you," she told him and poured two cups of coffee and brought out a plate of blueberry muffins.

"Mmmmm," he murmured. "Very tempting, these muffins, I might try just one, thank you."

"Do," she said with a twinkle, knowing that before he left he would have devoured all six of them. "Is Carstairs well?"

Bishop nodded. "But yearning for simpler days. He feels the CIA's becoming too big, too bureaucratic, too profligate and

12

rather arteriosclerotic, considering the global age we're into . . . Other than that he's the same brilliant and maddening Carstairs—but let's get down to Morocco."

"Do let's, yes," she agreed.

"All right, here it is," he said, "although before you agree to it, it's vital that you understand you'll be working for a very small department within the CIA, and quite separate, unacknowledged and known only to a few."

"Interesting," she murmured. "*Very* interesting but not yet intimidating . . . Go on."

"Good. We very much want—no, *need* you—to accompany a chap who'll be doing a job for us in Morocco. We had decided—once you said yes to going—that you travel with him as his aunt." He smiled appreciatively. "Aunt Emily Pollifax."

"Just—accompany him?"

He nodded. "There's not much else you could do in any case since you don't speak Arabic and you're a woman. The country's Moslem and the majority of women, especially in the rural areas, are seen but not heard, and if they're veiled they're really not seen at all. They live very separate lives, something to do with their Koran implying women are inferior."

Mrs. Pollifax sniffed indignantly.

"Janko's value," he pointed out consolingly, "is that he speaks Arabic . . . Max Janko, your companion."

She frowned. "Then if he speaks Arabic why does he need me?"

Bishop sighed. "It's all rather touchy, because he doesn't need you but we do. Carstairs has never met the man—Cairo chose him—but as you already know he's an expert on faces; Carstairs has these hunches about people that are positively psychic and I've never seen him wrong. This Janko chap is the only person available at such short notice who speaks Arabic, and this is important because you'll be traveling practically the length of Morocco, and it's hoped without being conspicuous and asking directions constantly. Actually Janko speaks Urdu, Chinese, Russian, Rumanian, and can translate Sanskrit as well," he added, "but as a person or personality Carstairs feels that he lacks—shall we say the courtesy or the sensitivity to get along really well in a Moslem country, the tact to insinuate himself out of any sticky situations that might develop?" He smiled. "Traveling with you—well, it's hoped that you'll be a nice auntlike influence so that if he should turn out to be a bull in a teashop, if he violates any customs or traditions of the country —loses his temper or is rude—you can smooth things over and in general keep an eye on matters. We are *not* into character assassination," he added, "but Carstairs is concerned, the job's important."

"Just what is this Mr. Janko to do?" she asked cautiously.

"Check out seven people," he told her, and digging into his briefcase he brought out a small envelope. "We felt it safest for you to deliver these to him personally. We've wired him your photo so he can meet you at the airport in Fez but we'd never have risked wiring these to him, we would have used a courier if you weren't joining us. These are photos we've not even shared with Cairo.

"Here they are," he said, handing her the envelope. "Seven snapshots, seven faces, each with an address on the back. Checking out each of these people will take you from Fez down into the southeast corner of the country so that you'll see quite a bit of Morocco. The real Morocco," he added brightly.

She looked at the envelope and then at Bishop. "May one ask who these people are?"

"Informants," he said.

"I see . . . surely there's more?"

He shrugged. "Certain rumors have reached us but I'm not

sure that Carstairs would feel they're anything to trouble your head about."

She said silkily, "My head likes to be troubled, Bishop."

"I know . . ." He thought a minute, hesitated and nodded. "All right, I'll say this: we've become alarmed that one of the seven people may not match his photograph."

Her eyes widened. "An imposter among your seven?"

"Yes," he added grimly, "Someone who may have taken over the identity of one of the people in the network—I shudder to think how—and who may be intent on corrupting, exposing or destroying the others in the network—and more than this, my dear Mrs. P., I am not at liberty to tell either you or Janko. Except to add," he said, "that you will travel by car from village to village, and Janko's instructions are to make no contact with any of the seven but to be quite certain each face matches its photograph, because names can be changed but not faces."

"Very true," she agreed, "but what if—"

"If there's a face that *doesn't* match," he went on, "you're to head for the nearest post office—"

"Post office?"

"Yes, in Morocco cables are sent from the government post office—not too easily found in the country you'll be driving through—and once you reach a hotel you'll verify your message with a telephone call to Baltimore, and since all long-distance calls go through Rabat, taking hours, we recommend discretion in what you report to us."

"Yes," she said, nodding. "And that's it?"

He smiled. "I think you'll find it challenging enough just to locate these seven people without anyone knowing what you're up to. That's where Janko's Arabic is so important. Two Westerners asking directions to an obscure person in an obscure village would be hellishly conspicuous and raise no end of trouble."

She found this logical and nodded. "And how will I recognize Mr. Janko?"

Bishop laughed. "You don't need to, he'll find *you*, but you can expect a man with—as Carstairs phrases it—a fierce black moustache and fierce black eyebrows and more than a soupçon of arrogance. However, if by any chance you should miss connecting at the airport in Fez he'll be at the Palais Jamai hotel and we've booked you a room next to his."

"The Palais Jamai," she repeated.

"I've also captured an Arabic phrase book for you," he said, reaching into his briefcase. "A French one, too, since Morocco was a French protectorate until 1956. But I think you'll find a fair number of people who understand English, at least in the larger towns and of course in Fez, and the phrase book has a nice little introduction to Morocco as well as a map." He dug deeper into his briefcase. "And here are your plane tickets— there are only three flights a week from Kennedy airport so be sure you're early—and here's Moroccan and American money, traveler's checks, your hotel reservation in Fez—after that you're on your own—and here's the usual cable address and phone number in Baltimore *if* . . ."

"If," she repeated gravely.

"Yes, if . . . We hope all is well but the information we've begun receiving through the pipeline has suddenly become rather garbled and simply doesn't check out with other available sources. Anything else? No, I think I've covered everything." He sat back, smiled at her and buttered his fourth blueberry muffin. "Any questions?"

"Yes," she said. "What's Morocco like?"

"Poor," he told her. "It all looked very promising after independence in '56 but now the country's been fighting a war for fourteen years that's costing it a million bucks a day so a lot of plans have been shelved. You'll find it poor."

"War?" she said in surprise. "With whom? What war?"

He reached over to the phrase book he'd given her and opened its pages to the map. "See this area in the south of Morocco?"

She nodded. "It's all yellow, which means desert, doesn't it?"

"Right. That's Western Sahara, about the bleakest and most inhospitable country anyone could fight over, but home to the people of the Sahara—the Saharans, mostly nomads—who have always lived there. It was a Spanish protectorate," he explained, "until Spain moved out in 1975, and at that time the Saharans were promised a vote of self-determination—a plebiscite under the United Nations—so that they could choose independence or alignment with another country. Unfortunately the vote was never held because Morocco immediately moved in to claim and occupy Western Sahara."

"That sounds rather greedy," murmured Mrs. Pollifax. "I take it the Saharans decided to fight?"

He nodded. "They're called the Polisarios, these people of the Western Sahara who have been fighting to get their land back for fourteen years. Actually they waged a pretty damn good guerilla war for a long time. Not from their own country —they had to abandon that—but from Algeria, which offered them humanitarian and military aid, and so they fight from a base in the Algerian desert around Tindouf." He said ruefully, "I might add that they've also waged a relentless war on the diplomatic front as well. They call themselves the Saharan Arab Democratic Republic—a country in exile—and are now bona fide members of the Organization of African Unity, and recognized by sixty-nine non-aligned countries . . . all this without a country."

"Do we recognize them, too?" she asked, puzzled. "The United States?"

He smiled faintly. "On the contrary, our government's been supporting Morocco in their war against them. We've been pouring money, equipment and advisors into Morocco, not to mention helicopters, tanks, air-to-ground missiles, ammunition and an electronic wall to keep the Polisarios out of Western Sahara."

At the look of astonishment on her face he said, "You weren't aware? I don't suppose many Americans inquire as to where their tax dollars go . . . a pity. Occasionally Congress has demurred at the cost but it's important on the theory that if the King of Morocco loses his war he could lose his throne; if he compromises and ends the war he could also lose his throne —there have already been several coup attempts—and he's preferable, as usual, to the unknown, right?" He smiled. "But I think we must dispense with the history lesson because what's important are the lives of seven people—or six, if one of them's a fake—but I did want to explain to you why the country's poor, and why it's advisable to keep a very tight hold on your purse—you'll find many beggars—and lock your door every night." He stopped, looking at her closely. "What's the matter, something wrong?"

"For me, yes," she said, nodding. "I don't think I can agree to this job after all, Bishop, I don't like the sound of it. After hearing about this my sympathies are quite frankly with the Polisarios, and an assignment to check out seven people who spy on them—" She shook her head. "I'm sorry, I simply can't."

He sat back and looked at her in dismay. "Damn it, I see I've been handling this very badly."

"I don't see how you could have handled it any better," she told him.

"All I did was explain why you should watch your purse—"

"Yes, and also *why.*"

"Which is where I went haywire and handled it badly." He ran his fingers through his hair, scowling. "Look here," he said, lifting his head and beginning again. "I'm under intimidatingly strict orders from Carstairs to tell you nothing more—it's for your safety as well as ours—and I *can't* tell you more. All I can say is, would you trust me if I tell you that this assignment could, given the right circumstances, *contribute* something to the conclusion of the war?"

She regarded him suspiciously. "I don't see how."

He sighed. "Well, I could point out that informants deal in information, and very often in information that governments try to conceal. I could, but inevitably it comes down to a matter of trust."

"Trust?"

"In Carstairs," he said, looking harassed and tense.

He had reduced it to its starkest simplicity and she thought this quite unfair but there was no evading the fact that she did trust Carstairs. She had grown to respect his integrity; he had never sent her knowingly into any assignment that might outrage her sensibilities and if he felt this trip actually contributed something to the end of a dreadful little war, then it was quite possible that it might.

She said warily, "You force me to admit that I trust Carstairs, yes."

Almost plaintively Bishop said, "Will you reconsider, then?"

He looked so miserable that she smiled. "I trust you, too, Bishop."

"Thank you."

"I have therefore reconsidered and I will go."

He drew a deep breath of relief. "Thank God," he said fervently. "You gave me some bad moments, you know, it's going to take me time to recover. Time," he repeated in a dazed voice, and glanced at his watch. "Oh damn," he exploded, "it's late, I've got to rush off, it's not only late but *I'm* late."

"You always have to rush," she pointed out.

"Well, I do a great deal of sitting when I'm back at headquarters but, once I leave, Carstairs saddles me with unbelievable lists and I'm due in Manhattan by 4 P.M." He glanced wistfully at the plate that had recently held six muffins and was now empty. "Jolly good, those muffins, it's a pity I have to go. But look here, you *will* squash Janko very firmly, won't you, if he goes around insulting people?"

She smiled. "I don't own an etiquette book but I'll encourage him to smile frequently."

"Lots of luck," he said dryly, and closed his briefcase with a snap. Leaning over he kissed her on the top of her head. "And bless you for saying yes, and a million thanks."

When Bishop had gone Mrs. Pollifax carried the envelope of snapshots upstairs, trying to recall what she knew of Morocco as she placed the photos on the bed next to her packed bags. She knew that the country occupied the upper left-hand corner of North Africa, with a coastline on both the Atlantic and the Mediterranean, and that Algeria was its neighbor on the east, and hadn't she also read that algebra had been invented in Morocco? *Or discovered or created, or whatever one does with algebra,* she thought crossly, having been thoroughly intimidated by the subject in her youth. She had of course seen and loved the film *Casablanca,* but Bishop had spoken only of Fez . . . and hadn't the Romans occupied North Africa long ago?

"But I've forgotten my history," she lamented, and seating herself on the bed beside the envelope of photos she surrendered to curiosity, removed the pictures and looked at them one by one, and then looked at each one again and finally spread them out on the bed so that she could study each face.

The photos had been thoughtfully numbered from one to seven. Arranging them in order and consulting the small map in the phrase book she learned the route that she and Janko would be taking through Morocco, and saw too how in each photo the scenery changed, moving from the narrow alleys in the old section of Fez to flat brown plains and a background of mountains, one of them capped with snow.

The snapshots of the informants were clear but she guessed they'd been taken by an amateur, and possibly without the knowledge of the informants because none of the seven looked posed, and only one of them had glanced in the direction of the camera. The faces also showed her what Bishop meant when he emphasized that Morocco was a Moslem country: she was looking at seven men wearing long robes, with three of the faces bearded; one of them wore a fez and the others wore turbans. Turning over each photo she found their names and addresses strange to an American ear: Hamid ou Azu, Ibrahim Atubi, Youssef Sadrati, Omar Mahbuba, Muhammed Tuhami, Khaddour Nasiri, Sidi Tahar Bouseghine, and she saw that they lived in towns called Er-Rachidia and Erfoud, Tinehir, Ourzazate Zagora, Rouida . . . Only their professions were familiar, with the exception of one who was, mysteriously, a bathhouse keeper; the others were, respectively, a seller of brassware, a cafe waiter, a hotel waiter, a shopkeeper, a barber and a carpet merchant.

She studied their faces for a long time but when she returned them to their envelope she didn't tuck them into her carry-on bag. Instead she began a search for the old money-belt that Cyrus treasured and had reluctantly replaced with a new one. She discovered it lying under his socks in a chest of drawers and found that her memory had been accurate: each of its three pockets was precisely the right size to hold snapshots. Discarding their envelope she fitted two photos into one pocket, two in the next, and three in the last: she would wear the money-belt to Morocco and not remove it until she could safely hand the photos to Janko.

She smiled, realizing that seven faces had turned into seven real people now, and that a commitment had been made.

Sunday

2. *During* the six-hour night-flight to Casablanca Mrs. Pollifax completed her homework. Although the snapshots remained securely hidden in Cyrus' money-belt she had copied on a sheet of paper the names and addresses of the seven informants and she spent an hour silently spelling out and memorizing them, and then another hour in checking the accuracy of her memory. When she was quite certain that seven names and addresses were indelibly engraved in her mind she tore the list into shreds and disposed of it in the lavatory; only then did she allow herself to sleep.

The plane beginning its descent toward Casablanca's airport roused her from an unsatisfying nap. A glance at her wristwatch told her that by New York time it was three o'clock in the morning but from her window she saw that far below in Casablanca the sun had long since risen and a bright and sunny morning was already under way. According to the announcement over the intercom it was eight o'clock now, and she set her watch accordingly and hoped that she was in time for her plane connection to Fez.

Two hours later, feeling rather battered by haste and the

confusion of languages, her second flight was landing in Fez and her thoughts had transferred themselves to the meeting with Max Janko that lay ahead. She realized that a certain tension had begun to intrude and that she was bracing herself for this first meeting with Carstairs' angry young man. Disembarking she moved through crowds of people waiting to greet friends and relatives, almost all of them chattering away in French, their faces running the gamut from black to beige to white, and nearly half of the men wearing fierce black moustaches.

But none of the fierce black moustaches approached Mrs. Pollifax.

She waited patiently, her two bags beside her. After waiting a full thirty minutes she found a counter with a young man standing behind it, and discussed with him the possibility of Mr. Janko being paged over the loudspeaker system but presently it became apparent that the young man thought she was looking for a Mr. Page, and at this point she gave up, carried her bags to the street, climbed into a taxi and asked to be driven to the Palais Jamai.

Her first impressions of the city through which they drove were vague: she was aware of a boulevard lined with trees and flowers, of narrower streets where the sun slanted across medieval walls with flaking paint, of here and there a balcony with delicate lacy grillwork, and there were certainly a large number of motorbikes abroad, but she was far more occupied with her emotions, which seethed. She was puzzled, tired, overstimulated, wary and not sure whether to be angry or philosophical about Janko not being at the airport to meet her. One must remain flexible, she reminded herself, but Bishop had implied that she would be met, and she saw no reason why she could not have been met . . . Drawing up to the Palais Jamai she thought it looked gloriously deluxe but for the moment she had no interest in its splendors; she only counted out dirhams to the driver of the cab and surrendered her two bags to a porter. Registering at the desk she inquired the number of Mr. Janko's room—it was 315—and after being escorted to room 314 she tipped the porter and went at once to 315 and knocked.

A man's voice called, "Yes, who is it?"

"Mrs. Pollifax, just arrived."

"Oh, good."

Steps could be heard, the door opened and Mrs. Pollifax was face-to-face with Janko. Cool eyes met hers measuringly, and in turn she measured him. A very confident young man, she decided, his erect posture and appraising glance told her that, as well as a look of arrogance that was startling. His eyes were shadowed by thick curly eyebrows almost as heavy as his glossy black moustache; he was dressed casually in jeans and an open shirt that did not at all match his air of formal coolness.

"Come in," he said, and having summed her up he looked amused.

She glanced around the room, noting an unopened and unpacked suitcase. "You've just arrived?" she asked, hoping this might explain her tiresome wait at the airport.

He didn't reply to this. He said, "Do sit down, you have the photographs, of course, but you're late, I expected you an hour ago."

She was surprised. She said politely, "I was told that you'd meet me at the airport. If I'm later than expected it's because I waited there."

His eyes rested on her without expression. "It was foolish of you to wait so long." As if aware of his coolness he smiled a very charming smile but she noticed that it didn't reach his eyes.

She said again, firmly, "I was told you'd meet me at the airport. You found it impossible?"

With a careless shrug he said, "I thought it entirely unnecessary."

"Then my being late," she told him reasonably, "ought surely to have been anticipated."

He looked a shade taken aback by this mild thrust, and shedding his coldness he smiled warmly. "Let us be done with this. If I offended you I am sorry but it was not given to me as a command to go to the airport, and there were certain things for me to do. Please sit down! You will accept my apology?"

"Of course," she said amiably, but she remained standing.

"Now if I may see the photographs, please," he said, extending a hand and waiting. "The photos with the names and addresses that you came to deliver to me. It is important that—" A knock on the door interrupted him and he called out impatiently, "It's not locked, come in."

It was a porter who opened the door and bowed. "The car has been delivered, sir, and I have come for your luggage."

"Yes yes," said Janko. "Tell them I'll be with them in five minutes but you can take my luggage now."

As the porter removed his suitcase Mrs. Pollifax looked at Janko with interest. "I begin to see why you overlooked my airport arrival," she said softly. "You plan to overlook me, too?"

The charm vanished. He said curtly, "I've been prepared to leave as soon as you deliver the photos to me." He hesitated and then said bluntly, "You might as well know I've no intention of taking you along with me, I'm accustomed to traveling alone. It's out of the question that I be accompanied—you can take a tour, do whatever you please, but leave me bloody well alone to do my job. The very thought of traveling with—with—"

"An aunt," she supplied helpfully.

"I have no aunts," he said, glowering at her from under fleecy eyebrows. "I wasn't consulted, this change was arranged entirely without my knowledge. The original assignment was simple, clear and without obstruction, and I don't know what the hell they're thinking of, saddling me with you. Do you speak Arabic? Have you any idea of the assignment or its importance, of how a second person can only slow me down or clutter up matters?"

She said coolly, "To that I can answer no, yes, no, no, and point out that better minds than yours, Mr. Janko, sent me here to accompany you."

"Better minds? That's insulting," he told her. "There's absolutely no need for you to be here once you've delivered the photos. I travel alone, damn it."

She said calmly, "I can understand your surprise at having an aunt foisted on you at the last minute, Mr. Janko—although I can certainly understand *why* now—but I'm sure you can also understand my surprise at finding you such a rude and unpleasant man. Obviously we must both make the best of a very unhappy situation."

"Impossible! I intend to do no such thing."

"You're very stubborn."

"No—independent," he flung at her. "Now hand over the photographs."

Mrs. Pollifax considered him thoughtfully. "I think not," she told him curtly, "in fact I see no other solution but to keep the photos, since as long as I have them I'm indispensable."

"You wouldn't dare!"

"Try me."

"Blackmail?"

She said pleasantly, "I believe it's called that, yes."

His eyes fell to her purse and she knew exactly what he was thinking; his glance moved around the room and then returned to her speculatively, and again she guessed his thoughts and braced herself; he was just furious enough to use force and she prepared to defend herself.

The moment passed, he shrugged and said curtly, "We're wasting time."

"Yes we are," she agreed, "since the first person to be checked out is here in Fez, in the medina."

He looked surprised. "In Fez?"

"Yes."

"Having established that, do you care to tell me where we go following that? If I'm driving, maps need to be studied and a route planned," he pointed out, adding sarcastically, "or do you plan to do that too?"

She said calmly, "The person we check out after Fez is in Er-Rachidia."

"Thanks," he said bitterly. Unfurling a large road map he examined it. "Then we head south, yes, but at Er-Rachidia there is a junction, you see?" He held out the map to her. "Beyond Er-Rachidia do we remain on route 32 and head west, or continue south to Erfoud?"

Unwillingly she said, "Erfoud."

"Good, Erfoud is a matter of 300 hundred miles and we should be able to drive that in one day. But not today," he said curtly. "I *suggest*," and here he used the word mockingly, "that we keep these rooms for the night and accomplish both Er-Rachidia and Erfoud tomorrow, unless, of course, you—?" He paused, lifting one eyebrow.

"There's no need to be sarcastic," she told him. "It sounds a very sensible and agreeable plan, especially since—" She looked at her wristwatch. "Especially since it's already afternoon now, and we have work to do here. If you'll excuse me I'll go to my room, change into walking shoes and be back in five minutes."

"I hope with the photos," he said.

"With one of them, yes." With a nod she left him, but his move from rage into mere sarcasm had not fooled her in the slightest, she was going to have to remain on guard. *How tiresome*, she sighed, but there was no overlooking the fact that for the briefest of moments he had actually been prepared to wrest the photographs from her by force. A strange man . . . she thought that only his doubts of their being in her purse had held him back but he would try again, of this she was sure; his outraged and affronted ego would not allow him to give up easily.

Entering her room she extracted from Cyrus' money-belt the snapshot labeled number one: Hamid ou Azu, a bearded man of middle age wearing a red fez and a striped djellabah. A shaft of sunlight illuminated his face and turned to gold the great bowls and trays of brassware that surrounded him in his souk. He looked a shrewd and prosperous businessman but she already knew his face, she had memorized it before leaving home, and the address on the back she had memorized on the plane:

Hamid ou Azu,
Place es Seffarin, in the medina Fès el Bali.
Fine brassware.

3. *After* what seemed to Mrs. Pollifax an interminable argument a guide named Dasran was hired for their trip into the medina. There was such a difference of opinion about this that Mrs. Pollifax realized there would probably be similar

arguments at every stop they made, and this further exacerbated her jet-lagged spirits. "The guidebook recommends—"

"Guidebook!" sneered Janko.

To this she pointed out that the Fès el Bali was centuries old, labyrinthian, and that finding one brassware merchant among all the souks in the medina would be very much like finding a needle in a haystack.

"You have a tourist mentality," he said scornfully.

Her reply was equally as hostile. "It's all very well to be a free spirit but it's already past one o'clock and there is such a thing as efficiency and getting the job done."

In the end she prevailed, and this at least gained her a reprieve because Janko glowered instead at Dasran, who wore a djellabah over Western clothes and beamed at them joyously. "Yes yes I take you to Place es Seffarin—much brass, much copper—come!"

They entered by the gate near to the hotel, the Bab Guissa, and plunged at once into another century, a medieval world of dim and cobbled alleys and passageways, and Mrs. Pollifax's spirits rose at once. Souk after souk lay before them on either side, lighted by a ray of sunlight from above, or by dim artificial light below, and if the interiors of the shops were like dark caves they nevertheless blazed with color: over one souk hung great skeins of brilliant silk thread—pink, fuchsia, purple, orange—suspended on ropes to dry. From the shop next door came the scent of perfume and of spices, with displays of magical wares: tree bark, roots, charms and potions. They passed souks with mounds of lemons, tangerines, oranges, black olives shaped into pyramids, and tubs of scarlet paprika, yellow saffron and cumin. Over it all hung a beehive hum of activity, of merchandise being made, bartered and sold. One turn in the twisting streets took them past woodcarvers, then a shirtmaker bent over his sewing machine. A stall sold lemonade and pastries next to a shop where sheepskins were being stretched taut over terra-cotta pots to fashion drums.

She and Dasran and Janko moved in a steady stream of people: old men in turbans and djellabahs shuffling along, pairs of women in black veils with only their eyes showing, and children who ran barefooted over cobbles slippery with damp and dung. In a particularly narrow and sunless alleyway a man behind Mrs. Pollifax shouted furiously *"Balek! Balek!"* and she flattened herself against a wall just in time to escape being trampled by a donkey with huge panniers strapped to its sides. The passage widened, a child raced past, saw them, stopped and held out a hand for money.

Dasran waved the child away but the incident appeared to have given him ideas of his own, for he turned to them, beaming. "You wish to see brass-work," he said. "My cousin—he sell beautiful brass pots—come see! Only a minute—in next street. Very good prices, too!"

Janko turned, lifting an eyebrow; he looked amused. "You asked for this," he said.

Thus challenged Mrs. Pollifax told Dasran sternly, "We wish the street of brassware. We wish to begin first with the merchant recommended to us at the hotel, the souk of Hamid ou Azu."

"Pah!" snorted Dasran. "You will pay dearly at that place, I can tell you. My cousin—"

She added firmly, "And we pay a very *large* tip to arrive there quickly. With haste."

She had only disappointed him for the moment. "A leather handbag? A beautiful leather handbag, surely? I have another cousin who sells beautiful Moroccan leather cheap."

"No."

He sighed. "How *much* tip?" he asked, weighing this

against the commissions he would receive from the shops of his cousins.

"Take us to Hamid ou Azu's shop and you'll see."

His shrug told her that he thought poorly of her for missing the wonderful purchases he was ready to present to her but he led them up and down alleyways until they arrived at an intersection, where he pointed to an open-fronted souk on the corner across from them. "There is the shop of Hamid ou Azu," he said indifferently, with a shrug.

And there he was, plainly visible to both of them, seated cross-legged before a low table and talking with a young man next to him who kept jabbing a finger at a pocket calculator. On the low brass table between them stood a tray with small glass cups of green tea.

They had found Hamid ou Azu, and his face exactly matched his photo.

Beside her Janko opened the guidebook in which he'd placed the snapshot she had given him, checked Hamid's face for himself and nodded. "Mission accomplished," he murmured. "Number one is in place." With a mocking glance he said, "You've found the shop, now I'll leave you to Dasran, I feel like a drink. You'll find me in the bar at the hotel."

She realized at once that he was enjoying a predicament that she'd not clearly foreseen when she'd insisted on a guide, and this was how to dispense with Dasran now that he'd brought them to the souk of Hamid ou Azu. Janko was gleefully abandoning her to solve this problem alone. She said silkily, "Yes, why don't you do that? Since Mr. ou Azu looks very busy with a customer I'll continue on with Dasran and buy a souvenir or two."

The glance Janko gave her came close to being appreciative, as if he suddenly found her almost a worthy opponent; then he turned and was quickly lost in the crowd.

To Dasran she said, pointing to his robe, "Show me a souk that sells djellabahs."

He brightened. "Djellabahs, yes."

"But no cousins, please."

Politely Dasran said, "That man—he is a little rude, is he not? Surely not your *ibn*—your son?"

"No—nephew."

When he looked puzzled she drew out her phrase book, turned the pages and pointed to herself. " *'amma.*"

"Ah," he said, nodding. "Not son—good! I not like him."

This immediately established a warmer relationship between them, since Mrs. Pollifax heartily agreed with his reaction to Janko—it was, after all, why Carstairs had sent her here—and she set out with him to explore more of the medina.

An hour and a half later, tired but happy, Mrs. Pollifax had bought a curved Moroccan dagger—a *khanjar,* Dasran told her—as well as a gray wool djellabah for Cyrus and a black-and-brown-striped one for herself. Over a cup of mint tea at a tiny cafe she learned that Dasran had three sons and a daughter, that times were not good, that he and his wife came from the Sous and that he would return Mrs. Pollifax to the hotel by way of the brassware souk but if she found the prices too high he would bargain for her.

"From my heart I do this," he said, "for the man is not a cousin. You are nice lady but—what is the word, innocent? To bargain you must begin low, very low. It is a game, you see? An enjoyment. It is how things are done here."

Mrs. Pollifax wanted to tell him that it was not necessary to return by way of Hamid ou Azu's shop, that in any case she was beginning to feel very tired and hungry but before she could explain this to Dasran he was on his feet, and soon she was being eagerly pushed through the crowds toward the Place es Seffarin. *Oh well*, she thought in resignation, *there may be something small to buy, and I will certainly enjoy meeting one of the informants.*

They emerged at the familiar intersection from which she had first seen Hamid ou Azu. The volume of sound had increased here, becoming more than the murmur of voices and the flip-flop of sandals treading over stone: she realized that someone was shouting loudly and insistently and that people had begun running.

Dasran abruptly clutched her arm, stopping her.

"What is it?"

"He says someone is dead."

"Dead?"

"He is shouting for teachers and for the *ulama* and for the police."

Watching the confusion she suddenly gasped, "But they're running to—Dasran, they're running to the shop of Hamid ou Azu! Something has happened, we must see what's happened." Shaking off his arm she raced across the cobbles to the growing swarm of people who had collected in front of the brassware souk. Pushing her way in among them she peered between heads and over shoulders and saw that a man had fallen across the brass table and that a knife had been thrust to the hilt into the flesh of his back. The face lay half-turned to the crowd, the eyes and mouth wide open; it was a face very familiar to her, and one that she had seen only two hours ago. It was Hamid ou Azu, and—*oh God,* she thought, *he's dead, he's been murdered . . .*

Dasran had edged to her side and was tugging at her sleeve. "Not to see," he told her, his face white with shock. "Bismallah, he is dead."

"Yes, dead," she whispered, and standing in this dim, medieval street of souks she felt a sudden chill run down her spine as she remembered that Hamid ou Azu was not just a merchant who sold brassware but an informer in a network of informers. She thought, *It's nonsense to think he's been killed for such a reason, he must surely have been an informer for years, why should he be killed now?*

Unless the imposter whom Carstairs suspected was already at work, she added, and shivered, wondering just what she had stumbled into with this assignment.

The crowd was retreating as a police car made its way down the narrow alley, pinning people to the wall to allow its passage. Feeling a little sick she told Dasran, "I hope it's not far to the hotel, I want to go there now." She realized that she felt astonishingly relieved that she was not on this trip alone, no matter how unpleasant her companion.

She found her unpleasant companion in the hotel bar, scowling into his drink. When she slid onto the stool beside him he glanced up and said, "I take it you managed to get rid of that vulture Dasran and I hope you didn't over-tip him."

"A small brandy—any kind," she told the bartender.

Looking more closely at her Janko said, "You look terrible, what's wrong with you?"

The brandy arrived, she drank half of it recklessly and felt the sickness in her subside. She said, "Hamid ou Azu is dead."

"*What?*" he roared, and then with a glance around him, "Sorry, but what the hell do you mean? How do you know such a thing?"

"Dasran and I started back to the hotel," she told him, her voice trembling only a little, "and we passed his shop on the way, and—and he'd just been killed. He was lying across a table with a knife in his back. A very *long* knife," she said, remembering.

His eyes narrowed. "You'd better finish that brandy."

"Yes, but do you suppose, do you think—?"

He sighed. "You have too melodramatic a mind. Rule number one is never leap to conclusions. A lot of these countries have blood feuds and long lists of wrongs to be avenged, and if what you're thinking—"

She finished the brandy and stood up, interrupting him. "What I'm thinking," she said, coldly, "is that we should leave *very* early tomorrow for Er-Rachidia and for Erfoud."

He nodded. "I'll meet you at five o'clock in the lobby downstairs."

Picking up her packages she left Janko, but not for her room. She went instead in search of Dasran, hoping he might be where they had found him stationed outside among the official tour guides who competed for tourists from the hotel. He was there, leaning against a car, his eyes hawklike in their search for business. When he saw her his face brightened. "Ah—my friend! You wish new tour? For you I give good price."

"No, Dasran, but I've a favor to ask of you," she said crisply. "About my nephew."

His face fell. "Oh—him."

"Yes." She said frankly, "He drinks far too much, Dasran."

He looked attentive but puzzled.

"He drinks *very* much," she emphasized. "His mother is very unhappy about this. She cries."

Dasran became all sympathy. "Ah, the *wiskee*, the wine . . . so that is why he is not nice."

"Yes. He tells me—he insists, Dasran—that he has *not* been at the hotel bar drinking ever since he left us in the medina." She sighed. "His mother is so upset about him. Could you cleverly—very quietly—ask the men who tend bar if he has been there since he left us? For learning the truth of this I will pay fifteen American dollars."

"*Madehm*," said Dasran simply, "for fifteen U.S. dollars I stand on my head."

35

"But only for the truth," she reminded him. "They will allow you to report to my room, which is 314?"

He beamed at her. "There are ways, *madehm*. Trust me, I will be there. Room 314."

Once back in her room she waited patiently, wondering many things, feeling a shade paranoid but wanting to cross her *t*'s and dot her *i*'s. Janko was CIA, but nevertheless Hamid ou Azu had been murdered today of all days and it remained a strange coincidence.

She might have waited patiently but when she heard the knock on her door she raced across the room to open it. Dasran stood in the hall looking very sad.

"I am so sorry, madehm," he said. "Sorry for his poor mother and for you. It was Madani Amar at the bar who served him, and he tells me—I am so sorry—he sat in the bar all that time, your nephew. More than one hour, nearly two. He drink five *beera,* one coffee."

"All that time? You're quite sure? This Madani is very sure?"

Dasran sighed mournfully. "He did not even go to the toilet, Madani says. Also Madani says he is not polite, he left no tip and he is sorry for his mother, too."

"Yes," she said with considerable relief, and counted fifteen dollar bills into his palm. "Thank you, Dasran."

"His mother will be very sad?"

"Yes she will be very sad," said Mrs. Pollifax, but she herself would not be. She might be traveling with a boor but at least she would not be traveling with a murderer.

She watched Dasran vanish down the hall and closed the door, feeling that she could now extract from Cyrus' moneybelt the photograph and address for the next day.

4 • *Mrs. Pollifax* slept, woke, slept and was awakened at 4:15 by the room service breakfast that she'd ordered. As she ate without appetite she remembered the dispiriting evening behind her when not even television—a James Bond film dubbed in French—had calmed her ruffled nerves. She had considered sending Carstairs a cable to personally report Hamid ou Azu's death, no matter what an affront to Janko this might prove to be; the idea was aborted, however, when a call to the front desk informed her that all post offices had closed for the day. This frustration had revived her stormy feelings about Janko, whose indifference to the murder appalled her, and for a fleeting moment she had experienced a very real panic at accompanying him for seven days. To be such an object of hostility was not something to which she was accustomed, and for that one moment she had longed to flee. Only a rush of anger at his insolence had dissipated the panic. She had bravely told herself that the hostility was his problem, not hers, and that she would not—must not—allow it to reach her and intimidate her or, worse, diminish her sense of self.

Nevertheless she had not slept well; her dreams had been haunted by a man lying across a brass table with a knife protruding from his back.

Promptly at five o'clock she was in the lobby with her bill paid and her bags beside her. In her purse she carried the photo and address of the informant in Er-Rachidia, which Janko had told her they would reach by early afternoon, and if they succeeded in finding him, and if he matched his photo there

37

would, by nightfall, be another informant to check out in Erfoud. She was taking no chances, however, and the Erfoud photograph remained securely in her money-belt. Reaching Er-Rachidia was enough for now—and by itself was a long drive —but in Er-Rachidia at the Gharbee Espresso cafe there would be—or so she hoped—a waiter named Ibrahim, a hearty-looking cheerful man, stocky and clean-shaven. In his photo he had stood with his hands on his hips, smiling, a line of outdoor cafe tables behind him, a green apron tied around his waist.

Janko emerged from the elevator a minute later to join her, gave her a curt nod and she followed him outside to the small blue Renault waiting for them. His first words were spoken in distaste. "What," he said, "is *that?*"

"This?" she said, handing him the package wrapped in newspaper. "Two djellabahs, bought yesterday in the medina." *Before the trip to the souks turned into nightmare,* she added silently.

He dropped the package into the trunk of the car as if she'd presented him with a day's supply of garbage, and she wished longingly that Cyrus was present: Cyrus would have dealt with Janko's rudeness with dispatch, as eventually she would have to, but then Cyrus' years as lawyer and judge had inured him to the less pleasant personalities of the world and he would probably only be amused.

I must try to be amused, she thought as she slid into the front seat of the Renault, and then a new thought struck her: would he act like this at all with Cyrus? was Janko's attitude due entirely to her being a woman?

It's possible that he feels humiliated, she thought in surprise, and this realization shook her, but she clung to it as a means of understanding him better.

"The photo now?" he asked with his usual sarcasm, holding out a hand.

She gave him the Er-Rachidia photograph. "We look for the Cafe Gharbee, on the main street."

With exaggerated politeness he said, "Thank you so much."

Starting the car they set off in the milky dusk that precedes sunrise, the sky steadily brightening until by the time they left Fez its buildings could be clearly seen and a golden light was slanting across rooftops and gilding the windows of white-washed houses. Janko drove in silence, keeping a wall between them as inpenetrable as Plexiglas. He simply did not want her with him and she felt that she could almost touch his antagonism, that it was becoming tangible, acquiring shape and substance, and both were oppressive. It had been suggested to her that he was arrogant but she'd not expected such a willful and lasting rejection of her presence and she found herself trying to remember why she was here at all. Certainly he was making it clear to her that she was of no use to him and that only a driver and seven photographs were needed for the job; he was refusing to discuss the tragedy yesterday in the medina and he was refusing even to discuss the weather, which was misty and cool. On this first morning in a strange country, with the man beside her such a determined stranger, the effect was palpable: she felt exiled and lonely.

What *was* she contributing, why *was* she here, she wondered, and struggled to remember Bishop's reasons for her assignment. *A leavening influence,* he'd said . . . *Carstairs is concerned* . . . and then something about smoothing over difficulties should Janko be rude or lose his temper. This struck her as rather hilarious now yet it comforted her as well, because so far Janko's rudeness had been directed only at her and at Dasran, but as they left Fez behind and headed into rural Morocco there would undoubtedly be other Dasrans at whom he could vent his contempt and then she would be of some use after all. *Rather like sweeping up litter behind someone who scatters it across the countryside,* she thought crossly.

To assert her presence she said boldly, "I understand that Morocco, being a Moslem country, considers women inferior to men, Mr. Janko. I wonder if it's possible, considering your attitude, that you also feel women are inferior?"

He gave her a quick glance. "Don't be tiresome."

"Would it be tiresome to comment on Hamid ou Azu's murder yesterday, too? It seems a coincidence that should concern us."

He shrugged. "That is entirely a matter for the police."

"Yes, but if we—do you think it possible we're being followed, and that perhaps we led the murderer to him?"

He pointedly adjusted the rear mirror and looked into it. "There is no one following us, and why should they? You imagine too much."

She too glanced back but the road was empty and she sighed, wishing him more approachable. "What about the weather then, which begins to be colder than I expected?"

"I despise small talk," he said.

And that was that . . . it seemed useless to continue but she thought one more day like this and she would no longer be able to contain her anger, and she would scream at him, and she had not screamed in years.

Their route out of Fez had taken them past the King's palace—one of seven, her guidebook told her—its gates well guarded by men in dark olive uniforms and bright green berets decorated with scarlet insignia. Once they left the city behind, however, they entered a countryside almost empty of people. They drove between lush green fields under a great pale sky, the terrain flat to the horizon and the only signs of habitation a few ancient crumbling walls and suddenly a tiny country store in the middle of nowhere, with bricks placed on its corrugated tin roof to defend it against the winds that swept across the valley.

Presently stands of sharply pointed cypress trees appeared, softening the flat green landscape, and a smudge of mountains could be seen far, far away to interrupt and promise change. Mrs. Pollifax felt a stab of longing for Cyrus with whom she could compare notes: a drive of three hundred and fifty miles with Cyrus could never be dull, his comments were always pithy and frequently humorous, and being captive with him in a car was pure delight.

She thought, *Until now I've met such wonderful people— such interesting people—on these trips for Carstairs, and I mustn't complain because the law of averages has caught up with me, I've simply been very fortunate in the past.* She found herself remembering John Sebastian Farrell with whom she had shared her first adventure in Albania, and then another in Zambia, and she smiled as she thought of that dear, swashbuckling man. There had been so many others, too, like Robin Burke-Jones whom she'd first met as a cat burglar in Switzerland. The notes and cards that arrived each Christmas bore such exotic stamps that she'd had to deflect the postman's curiosity by giving him the stamps for his son's collection, but it had proven *very* difficult to explain the envelopes with the royal crest of Zabya.

They were passing the first village she'd seen in an hour, a small compound of flat-roofed adobe houses. Men in shabby djellabahs and boots stood around a huge steaming pile of manure while two men shovelled it into donkey-drawn carts. The gate in the wall behind them was a faded blue, it was half-open and a barefooted child stood watching the men, and then they were leaving the village behind, the earth was turning chocolate-brown and power lines began to appear along the road. Small hills rose ahead of them to block the horizon and then—abruptly—the road curved and a mountain of stone lay ahead, combed with caves, its southern slope green with lichen and grass.

They were climbing now, and with their ascent into a higher altitude the landscape changed to one of rocks and grass against a backdrop of mountains and a sky filled with great drifting horizontal clouds. To her surprise Janko cleared his throat and spoke. "Middle Atlas," he said with a gesture toward the mountains ahead.

"Thank you," she said politely, and to encourage conversation added, "Have you visited Morocco before, then?"

He said deflatingly, "No—I simply brought a very good map."

"I see." Trying again she said, "If we've several hundred miles to drive, have you decided where we'll find a place to lunch?"

He said stiffly, "The next town of any size is Midelt, we'll stop there."

"Good," she said, and they returned to silence, but she could not help wondering what he thought about as he drove; at times she saw his brows draw together in a frown and once the the corners of his heavily moustached lips had deepened in an actual smile. His thoughts, she decided peevishly, must be very entertaining indeed; it was a pity that he refused to share them.

They lunched in Midelt in a cafe with round tables and red chairs and grimy windows, sharing a *tajine* that was brought to them steaming, its large clay pot heaped with couscous, stewed pumpkin, cabbage, lentils and shreds of chicken. If they lunched in total silence there were at least people whom Mrs. Pollifax could watch: there was a young European girl seated at a small table with a packet of Kiri cigarettes in front of her, and a pot of mint tea; she stared calmly into space with the smoke of her cigarette curling around her. In one corner there huddled a group of sullen-looking workers and near them a small party of tourists who seemed to be speaking German. The clock on the wall advertising a famous cola had long since stopped, its hands fixed at nine. She carefully read the advertisements pasted on the walls for Stork Beer and NIDO ("instant full cream powdered milk from Nestlé") and for Sidi Harazem Eau Minérale Naturelle.

She was almost sorry to leave but her interest was quickening now in the remaining miles, because by mid-afternoon they would be reconnoitering informant number two, followed by number three in the evening. If they continued at such a rapid pace, she thought with relief, her assignment would be completed earlier than anticipated and her dreary companion relegated to the attic of her memory, like the new variety of geraniums that had defeated her best efforts three summers ago, and were only distantly recalled.

Ahead of them, leaving Midelt, lay a brown and rocky landscape with strange volcanic-shaped mesas silhouetted against distant snowcapped mountains. They passed a few houses built of round stones with tin roofs, then a village of adobe that boasted a minaret and a Moroccan flag blowing in the wind, its scarlet the only note of vivid color in the somber countryside. Always she was aware of their climbing higher into the Mid-Atlas; there were actually patches of snow on the barren ground now to prove it. The rocks—of every possible shade of copper—turned next into towering hills pockmarked with caves; they skirted a deep gorge, passed through a tunnel carved out of the rocks and emerged into a welcoming sunshine.

To Mrs. Pollifax the town of Er-Rachidia looked an oasis of civilization after their long trip through such empty brown landscapes. They drove down a wide main street lined with doorways bearing the signs *Dentiste, Bureau de Poste, Docteur, Tabac, Tailleur;* there was even a canopied wagon at an intersection with a man selling sweets. The sun shone, and in every direction she looked there were mountains rising level after level toward the faraway snowcapped peaks of the High Atlas, so that the town seemed to be cradled among hills. Her spirits revived at once. The worst was over, they had reached Er-Rachidia, and their next and last stop, Erfoud, lay only eighty or ninety miles beyond.

To further nourish her enthusiasm she saw the Cafe Gharbee almost at once, halfway down the main street and facing the intersection that was the center of town. "There it is!" she told Janko eagerly. "The outdoor cafe on the right, and doesn't it look charming!"

He said testily, "I'm quite capable of finding it without help."

"I didn't doubt that for a moment," she said, refusing to allow him to squash this rebirth of spirit. There were actually cars here, too, the street was lined with them but where had they all come from, she wondered, after their seeing so few on the roads? Parking looked difficult until a tiny car with a sign *Petit Taxi* pulled out from a space close to the cafe. Janko slid the Renault into it and turned off the engine.

"I'll treat," she said magnanimously. "Mint tea or espresso?" Without waiting for his reply or even for him to join her she opened the door and hurried ahead, delighted to be away from him for a few seconds, to be free, to breathe in the crisp mountain air and to walk again before her legs became immutably frozen into a sitting position. She chose a table near the door the cafe where she could look into the interior as well as watch people passing on the street, and a moment later she was joined by Janko.

"Not as many djellabahs here, quite a few slacks and Western T-shirts," she murmured.

"Provincial capital," he said shortly.

"Oh."

From her chair she could see no one resembling Ibrahim, or any waiter at all, and she decided it was an appropriate time to find a ladies' room. Janko was yawning and she realized that he was human after all: a drive of nearly three hundred miles, with a stop only for lunch, was having its effect upon him.

Inside the cafe a few men were seated at the counter where tea and espresso and beer were dispensed. Tending this bar was a heavily moustached older man but he was not Ibrahim Atubi. It occurred to her that if they discovered the imposter here in Er-Rachidia she could not imagine Janko being anything but a liability: would his antagonism toward her, for instance, interfere with their orders to cable Baltimore at once, would his obsessive refusal to share the assignment with her outweigh the purpose of their assignment? This thought was new to her and it troubled her.

She emerged from the ladies' room, nearly colliding with a man rushing down the hall with a tray. He wore a green apron tied around his middle and he stepped back with a hasty, "Pardon, madame!"

She looked at him and smiled: she had nearly run into Ibrahim. "It's perfectly all right," she told him.

"Ah, you speak English! Has your order been accepted?"

"We're outside," she said.

He nodded vigorously. "One minute and I shall be there, madame. Excuse me, there was need for more—how you say—buns?"

"Buns, yes," she told him, and retraced her steps to join her companion at their table outside. Janko had lit a cigarette and returned to whatever thoughts had been diverting him all day, his heavy brows knit together in a frown.

Ibrahim followed, and with a bow and a smile that precisely matched his photo he inquired what they would like.

Janko, giving him a long and thoughtful glance, said, *"Du thé à la menthe."*

"Espresso," said Mrs. Pollifax, and as he left she smiled at Janko. "We have met Ibrahim."

He nodded. "Yes, we have met Ibrahim."

"Very pleasant man."

He shrugged. "No doubt."

Their drinks were brought to them: for Janko a tray holding a glass of tea filled with sprigs of mint on a plate ringed with cubes of sugar, and for her a tiny cup of espresso. Her cup was quickly emptied and since there was to be no conversation she glanced at Janko, who sat without expression, taking occasional sips of his tea. *Two solitudes side by side but never touching,* she thought—such waste—and with a glance at her watch she said, "I've finished my espresso, I'm going to walk up that street over there and see a little of Er-Rachidia. I won't be long."

"Don't be," he said curtly.

She rose and crossed the road to the opposite street, passing under a sign *Dentiste* that displayed a menacing picture of teeth. She paused beside a kiosk of magazines and newspapers and smiled at a Mickey Mouse book entitled *Mickey Jeux,* discovered no English newspapers and continued on to the next shop, which was hung with gaudy paper garlands of red and yellow and turquoise. Its sign read *Tabac,* a smaller one read *Souvenirs.*

She entered, nodding to the owner behind the counter, and began a happy browsing among its merchandise. There were small polished boxes of cedarwood, packages of incense and candles for the mosque, primitive carvings of stone and several unusual brass-and-silver cases, one of which she picked up to examine and admire.

A voice behind her said in English, "What you hold is a box to contain the Koran—as you see, it has a cord attached to wear it around the neck."

The English was flawless. She turned to find the owner still behind the counter but a new customer beside her, a man in a gray-and-white-striped djellabah, his dark head-scarf loosened to show an amiable and attractive dark face with a thin moustache and—surprisingly—a pair of blue eyes.

"Thank you, I didn't know," she said, smiling at him.

He called something to the owner in Arabic and was answered. In a low amused voice he said, "He tells me the price is forty-five dirhams but—if I may advise—if you find it charming and care to buy it, try bargaining."

Her relief at talking with someone, and being talked to, was profound; she was being regarded as a human being at last, and she was moved by his friendliness. "I think it's *very* charming," she said, beaming at him. "Do you care to take this one step further and suggest what I offer him?"

"Try thirty-five dirhams."

"Oh dear, what's that in dollars, would you happen to know?"

"Roughly $4.50, I believe."

"So little!" she marvelled, and entering into the moment she called out to the owner, "Will you accept thirty-five dirhams for this?"

The man behind the counter gently upbraided her blue-eyed companion, shrugged dramatically, sighed and at last smiled. "Oui—yes. Thirty-five dirhams."

"There, you see?" said her new friend, and added, "Are you on tour, have they told you about Er-Rachidia? The people here are called the Shrine People, descendants of Ali. It is a very special place."

"I didn't know that, either," she told him, smiling and sorting through her coins. "This is a dirham?"

"Yes—no, not that one, only the large coins, but you've not enough of them. You have bills? Ah yes, there are your thirty-five dirhams."

"How would I say 'thank you' in Arabic?" she asked.

"You would say *shukren*."

She nodded. "Then to you I will say thank you, and *shukren* to him." Presenting her bills to the shop's owner he wrapped her Koran box in newspaper, tied it with string and presented it to her.

"Shukren," she told him, smiling.

"You learn our language!" he said, delighted.

With a wave at The Man With The Blue Eyes she hurried out of the shop, and looking toward the cafe saw Janko standing impatiently beside the car waiting for her. But she was returning contented; she had actually spoken with two natives, she had made a small connection with this country and perhaps she could make something of this trip after all.

Her contentment was soon dispelled; Janko was tight-lipped and furious. "We have almost ninety more miles to drive," he said angrily, "and you delay us, just as I predicted. Need you be reminded you are not here for sightseeing and shopping?" When she simply stared at him, appalled by the tone of his voice he extended one hand and said, "I would like to see *all* the photographs now, I think you've been childish long enough about this."

Her own lips tightened. "Childish?" she repeated. "Mr. Janko, I have a temper, which I shall presently lose if you continue to act like this, because a great deal of rage is building in me at your attitude and at your—your positive *greed* over those photos. You are turning what could be a pleasant journey through Morocco into a very unpleasant trip."

"Now you prove your naivete and your inexperience," he told her coldly. "Agents are trained never to express emotions and you have already lost your temper."

"On the contrary," she retorted, "I have not even *begun* to lose it."

"I can't wait," he snapped, and opened the car door for her. "Get in, we've wasted enough time." Without renewing his demand for the photos he climbed into the driver's seat and started the car.

We are now reduced to quarreling, she thought bitterly, and said no more. Glancing toward the cafe she saw that Ibrahim had begun clearing their table, and hearing the sound of the motor he looked up, saw her and waved.

Returning his wave she thought, *If just once in a while I can meet people like Ibrahim and The Man With The Blue Eyes, then I may find it tolerable accompanying Janko.* But she knew that she had encountered one of the more devastating kinds of loneliness in existence: that of being in close contact with someone to whom she was a nonperson, and who thereby rendered her invisible and of no consequence.

As Janko gunned the engine there came to her through the open window of the car the distant chant of a muezzin, the rise and fall of a stern and ululating voice as it called the faithful to prayer—*Allah Akbar! Allah Akbar!*—and then the voice faded in the wind and with a squeal of tires the car pulled out into the main road to head next for Erfoud where they would end this day. But there was satisfaction in knowing that informant number two had been found and identified, and that before the day ended they should be able to identify informant number three, the young hotel waiter named Youssef Sadrati.

It was dark when they reached Erfoud, and it had grown cold, very cold, so that when Mrs. Pollifax walked into the hotel she was wrapped in sweaters and shivering, ready for bright lights and a warm room. Her endurance was not to be rewarded, however, for the lobby of the hotel was sparsely furnished and dimly lit. Janko stood back while she registered and was assigned room 306, and presently a bent little man appeared, picked up her bags and led her through a labyrinth of cold cement halls, turning right and then left, the halls so dark she felt as if she was being guided through catacombs. Their destination turned out to be a courtyard in the rear whose centerpiece was a swimming pool still filled with water. At each corner of the pool a sunken lamp emitted feeble rays to interrupt the darkness and this ghostly illumination gave the water a sinister and metallic gleam so that it looked alive, with a faint subterranean movement as if made restless by some terrible secret concealed in its depths. Rows of doors surrounded the pool, each with a window next to it.

"It's certainly very dark," she confided to her escort. *And spooky,* she added silently, but he spoke no English and only nodded as he inserted a key into the lock of her door. She gave one more glance at the water lying sullenly behind her, and with a shiver walked into her room to meet what she guessed was a 25-watt light that illuminated a bed, a chair, a shelf and a small bathroom beyond.

She tipped the porter, thanked him, and when he had gone she hurried to the window to draw the curtain and hide the dark courtyard with its dull glistening water. She thought it possible that at another season this hotel might have some charm but at the moment it held the atmosphere of a deserted summer camp. There was neither television nor telephone in her room, the silence was tomblike and the thought of retracing her steps to find the dining room depressed her even further. Nevertheless she was hungry and sensibly concluded that a meal would cheer her flagging spirits. Pausing only to comb her hair she set out again, encouraged by glimpses of light escaping from a few drawn curtains as she passed them. With relief she reached the lobby; no ghostly hands had reached out from the hall's alcoves to grasp her, she had met with no one in the darkness and yet she still felt oddly pursued. To restore her sense of competence she went immediately to the bar and ordered a bottle of mineral water with which to brush her teeth. Carrying it with her she marched into the adjacent dining room and was astonished to find it brightly lighted and occupied by a large party of tourists seated at a long table.

"Madame is in the party from France?" asked a young man hurrying to meet her.

She turned to look at him. He wore the waiter's uniform of black trousers, a black vest that was too tight for him, black tie and white shirt. He was clean-shaven, with an eager brown face and soft dark eyes, and seeing him she smiled brilliantly at him because he was Youssef Sadrati, she had found him, he was here and operative. She longed to address him by name, shake his hand, tell him that she had carried his photograph with her all the way from America but she only shook her head. "No, I'm alone," she told him.

He led her to a table and explained why he could not present her with a menu. "There is only a tajine tonight," he said apologetically, with a gesture toward the party of tourists. "So many!"

She smiled. "Then I will have tajine, yes."

"Thank you, madame," he said with considerable relief, and headed for the kitchen.

A minute later Janko entered the dining room and took a table in an opposite corner; presumably he had seen Youssef and satisfied himself as to his identity. He did not look at her nor did she look at him again. She sat and patiently waited for her tajine and watched her dinner hour slowly turn into nightmare because she sat for thirty minutes before her dinner arrived and then it was cold; a tyrant of a headwaiter loudly harangued his waiters and the group of tourists grew noisier and noisier. Mrs. Pollifax had reached the plateau of dessert when the headwaiter impatiently wrested a tray of glassware from a waiter who moved too slowly, then tripped and fell to his knees, littering the floor with broken glass; nightmare had turned into farce. Suppressing a somewhat hysterical laugh she finished her flange, stumbled back through long dark halls again and with relief entered her room where she brushed her teeth, undressed and fell exhausted into bed.

She had been asleep for a long time when she was awakened by the small but insistent sound of someone fumbling with the lock on her door. She did not move. It was too dark to see the door open but when she felt a sudden draft of night air across her face she knew that her room had been entered; the faint click of the door's closing confirmed it.

Bishop had warned her about thieves but she did not think her intruder a stranger. Back in Fez she had suspected this possibility: determined to gain the photographs, Janko was choosing tonight to rob her of them.

5. *Tense* and watchful she lay in bed and rued the care with which she'd closed the curtains at the window: not so much as a splinter of light entered the room, which made it necessary for her to rely on instinct and hearing alone. Using both she guessed that her intruder had reached the shelf that served as a desk and on which her two bags stood, and a moment later this was confirmed when a pencil-thin light shone briefly across the wall before it disappeared inside the blue khaki bag that held her clothes. He had been careless in turning on his flashlight too soon—it had outlined his profile, leaving no doubt of his identity—but he was not careless a second time, he worked in the dark. Listening, she closed her eyes, surprised by the atavistic sensitivity that could still be brought into play in the twentieth century: it was easier to listen with her eyes closed, it concentrated her hearing exclusively on sound, on the infinitesmal whisper of cloth moving against cloth, the rustle of an envelope being opened in her second bag, a small intake of breath as Janko found a photograph, and the expulsion of breath as he learned the photo was of an American male. There was the slow, nearly soundless unzipping of pockets at the side of each carry-on bag, and then his move to the left to investigate the small bathroom.

She winced as she understood that he would look next for her purse. Long ago she had adopted the habit of keeping it very near her on her travels in case of just such an occurrence, and tonight it was on the floor next to her bed within easy reach of her hand. If he found it and risked looking through it for the photos she thought this would present her with certain interesting choices: she could either continue to feign sleep or she could deliver a good sound karate chop to his head, which would render him unconscious and was precisely what he deserved. It was wonderfully tempting to consider a karate slash as he knelt beside her bed. and she thought about it with enthusiasm. She could explain later, very innocently, "I'm so terribly sorry, I assumed you were a burglar!" It would scarcely improve a wretched relationship but what a marvelous way to vent some of the anger that she was repressing!

But then what?

She sighed as she relinquished such a delicious idea; she reminded herself that Carstairs had assigned them both to this job, they were co-agents, and the job not half done yet, and of course Janko would be furious at being discovered in her room and even more furious at being hit over the head, and they would still have to work together. She thought with regret that it was a great pity but really she must abandon the idea.

He had finished his brief search of the bathroom now and was back in the room again. She sensed him moving closer and guessed that he had dropped to the floor to begin a stealthy approach to her bed and the thought of him on hands and knees struck her as suddenly ludicrous and she had to suppress a laugh. Soon she heard his fingers grasping her purse and slowly, softly opening it, and with eyes not entirely closed she became aware of that same pinpoint thread of light as he examined its contents.

Enough, she decided, and with a few appropriate murmurs turned over in bed, coughed gently and turned over again.

She had startled him, and she felt a jarring of the bed as he lifted his head so abruptly that he bumped it against the bed-frame. This was followed by a muffled gasp and then silence as he waited, listening. When he was satisfied that she'd heard nothing and was still asleep he rose to his feet and tiptoed to the door; a moment later the door opened and silently closed behind him.

It was over.

She was up at once, wide awake and released from all pretense of sleep but not from her sense of outrage at this invasion of the night. Reaching for her own tiny flashlight she groped her way to the bottle of mineral water on the shelf, poured herself a full glass and stood in the darkness sipping it and thinking, her anger mounting as she thought of his being so obsessed over the photographs that he would try to steal them while she slept.

There was also the realization—but it occurred to her only now—that Janko had not left entirely defeated: he had left with the knowledge that she'd not concealed the photos in either of her two bags or in her purse, and therefore they would have to be on her person.

And that was MY *mistake,* she thought, *I should have started mumbling in my sleep before he reached my purse and certainly before he finished his search of it.*

Knowing this, what would he do next to wrest them away from her?

But what challenged her most of all as she stood there in the darkness was *why* he was so insistent about the photographs. There was his monstrous ego, of course, and his anger at her being assigned to join him . . . were either enough to explain his actions tonight?

She did not dare turn on a light that might subtly illuminate the curtain and seep through to the walkway outside. Trusting to the thin beam of her pocket flash she opened her blue carry-on bag and extracted a book to calm her, and turned back to bed. As she moved toward it the dime-sized beam of light fell upon something small and furry next to the bed, not far from her purse, and she gasped, suppressing a cry of alarm.

But the furry object didn't move, it didn't scurry away at her approach and when she cautiously knelt beside it she found that it was not a small animal at all. It lay there lifeless, small, black and—puzzled, she picked it up and discovered that it wasn't fur, it was *hair*.

Baffled, she carried it into the bathroom, closed and secured the door behind her and risked turning on the dim overhead light. The object she held measured roughly one and a half inches long by an inch wide; the hair was black, healthy and thick and it was affixed to a rough sort of cloth which held remnants of adhesive. The revelation of what this had to be filled her with astonishment.

She was holding one half of a man's moustache.

It was this that Janko had left behind, apparently jarred loose when his head bumped the bed.

Her reaction was swift; she quickly turned off the light and retraced her steps to the bed where she dropped Janko's moustache on the floor again as if it were a live and ticking bomb— and indeed it was, she admitted as she sat down on the bed to calm and marshall her turbulent thoughts and consider what this meant. The ramifications seemed to her quite grave. If her first thought was *he mustn't know I've seen this,* and her second thought was *how soon will he return for this,* she knew that she was only avoiding the third and most crucial question of all: *If Janko's moustache was false, how much else about him was false?*

If his moustache was a fake, were those ridiculously heavy brows of his false, too, and where were these questions taking her, and why was there a chill running down her spine? She groped her way back to the beginning of this, to a Janko so insulted by her joining him in Fez that only her refusal to hand over the photographs had prevented her being dismissed and left behind. For some important reason it had been imperative for him to travel alone, and it had been equally important for him to gain those photographs, his need so acute that he'd now been reduced to robbery.

And the moustache he wore was false. *Why?*

And now, with a nearly heart-stopping sense of shock she returned to the terrible death of Hamid ou Azu.

Oh come now, Emily, she protested, *what you're thinking is insane, he was drinking beer at the bar in the hotel during those two hours, remember? Furthermore this is a man cleared and assigned by Carstairs and his department, he has the right name, he*

56

was in the right place and at the right time, and he expected a Mrs. Pollifax . . .

But it wasn't insane, of course, and she knew it. Hamid ou Azu was the first informant in a network of seven they'd been sent to check out; together she and Janko had found and identified him, and then they had separated. She could not explain the four beers in the hotel bar but she could no longer dismiss the coincidence—not now—when ninety minutes later Hamid ou Azu was mysteriously dead with a knife in his back, and if she and Dasran had not returned by that same street in the medina she would never have known of his death. Or his assassination.

Who was Janko working for?

She was aware of her mind frantically attempting to rationalize away a murder that could still be coincidence; she wanted to blot out the horror of her suspicions but nothing explained away her terrible unease.

Had Janko betrayed his superiors? Was he working with or against her?

And waiting for her still was the awfullest possibility of all: *If Janko had somehow returned to the medina in Fez yesterday and killed Hamid ou Azu—if her fifteen U.S. dollars had not bought her the truth—then what about Ibrahim, the second informant whom they'd verified that afternoon in Er-Rachidia?*

She thought, *I must telephone from here to the Cafe Gharbee in Er-Rachidia. I'll ask to speak to Ibrahim . . . I'll tell whoever answers that I left something behind yesterday, a kerchief, a scarf . . . I'll explain that only Ibrahim would remember, would know . . .*

And he will come to the phone, she added, *and I will be reassured and everything will be all right.*

She glanced at her watch and saw that it was 5 A.M.—too early—surely it would be better to wait until six o'clock? But in any case, and no matter what news her phone call brought, it

57

was time now to make certain that Janko never gained the snapshots he was so bent on retrieving.

Removing the money-belt from under her pajamas she opened its pockets and drew out the remaining four photos. Extracting a book of matches from her travel kit she walked into the bathroom and placed the snapshots on the sink. She had studied and memorized them at home and on the plane but just to be sure she closed her eyes and whispered again the names and addresses: of Omar Mahbuba who could be found selling fossils and various tourist items in a tiny shop below a certain tourist hotel in Tinehir . . . Muhammed Tuhami the barber in the old section of Ourzazate . . . Sidi Tahar Bouseghine, a seller of fine carpets in Zagora, and Khaddour Nasiri the bath-house keeper in the last town, Rouida, at the edge of the desert. Opening her eyes she held each one to a lighted match, set fire to them and watched them slowly curl under the heat. When they had been reduced to ash she ran the faucet hard into the basin and saw their remains swept away.

The job completed she heard a rooster crow outside the bathroom window, signalling the official dawn. Quickly she dressed in slacks, sandals and sweater and repacked her bags. Assuming that Janko would have no difficulties in picking her lock again to retrieve his moustache she locked it behind her, surprised to face a cold and drizzly morning. It was already six o'clock when she walked the long dim corridors to the lobby and found a man on duty at the desk.

"I want to place a call to Er-Rachidia, to the Gharbee Cafe," she told him.

He looked at her curiously. "Yes, of course—an 057 area, so it will take a few minutes."

"I'll wait," she said.

He carried the phone to the smaller counter on the side and began talking into it, rather sharply she thought, his fingers tapping the counter impatiently. She saw him reach for a memo pad and write down a number, and just as he picked up the phone again she glanced toward the dining room as its doors were opened by the headwaiter. Beyond him Youssef was carrying a tray of cups to the long table near the door. As he set down the tray she reached a decision, and gave in to the impulse that swept her. To the man at the desk she said, "I'll be right back," and walked across the lobby, entered the dining room and strolled over to Youssef.

In a normal voice, "What time do you begin serving breakfast?"

He smiled, bowed, said, "We serve now, madame."

In a low voice she said quickly, "I must tell you that if you know the name of Hamid ou Azu in Fez—"

His eyes widened and he sucked in his breath audibly.

"—he has been murdered. Killed. In his souk."

Youssef turned white. "Who are you?" he gasped.

So he knew the name of Hamid ou Azu . . . She said grimly, "The hand of fate."

"*Shukren*—I go," he whispered.

"Go fast," she told him, and aware that she was being summoned back to the desk she hurried across the lobby to the phone that was held out to her. Grasping it she said, "Cafe Gharbee? Do you speak English?"

"Yes, yes, a little. What is this?"

"I wish to speak to Ibrahim, the cafe waiter—he served me espresso yesterday and—"

She was interrupted. "Ibrahim? Not here."

"Later?"

"Not later."

"When, please?" she demanded.

"I am sorry, madame," said the voice. "We do not know

59

why—it is most sad—but the police took him away yesterday. A good man, too."

Police, she thought, shocked. Hamid ou Azu dead and Ibrahim arrested . . . She said, "But please, why—"

A hand suddenly reached out from behind her and cut the connection. Janko said smoothly, "Good morning, *aunt*—you are attempting a long-distance call?"

She spun around in anger to find his eyes blazing at her with fury. "That was rude of you," she said, and saw that he was fully moustached now.

To the man at the desk Janko said, "You will kindly tell me who my—my *aunt* was phoning?"

Mrs. Pollifax said sharply, "Don't, this is a private matter."

The desk man looked from one to the other, perplexed.

"Tell me," repeated Janko with authority.

The man said, "It was a call to Er-Rachidia, to a cafe named Gharbee."

"Yes," said Mrs. Pollifax indignantly. "I left my scarf there, my very best one, it must be there, it's missing."

Ignoring this Janko said curtly, "Prepare our bill, please, and send a man to my aunt's room 306 for her bags. We will not stay for breakfast."

Mrs. Pollifax said hotly, "I insist on breakfast!"

The manager had turned away to summon a porter. In a low voice Janko said, "You will insist on nothing, I am holding a gun at your back, not visibly because it is in my pocket but my hand is also in my pocket ready to pull the trigger if you don't walk at once to the car."

Mrs. Pollifax thoughtfully considered this command. It had always distressed her that so frequently the threat of a gun cowed people into early submission, and that in some cases it was kinder to risk being shot in public than to be carried off to an uglier death in private. She was very tempted to call Janko's bluff and defy him, finding it difficult to imagine him using the gun—if it was a gun—in a public place with witnesses. The attention of the police would be disastrous. Unfortunately, however, she knew that she was denied the luxury of choice. She had accepted this assignment and it was a commitment, and she mustn't think of home and Cyrus now but of four lives it was her job to save—*Insh'Allah*, she thought wryly—for she must learn *why* Hamid had been murdered, and why Ibrahim had been taken away, either by genuine police or by men masquerading as police. Above all she had to learn why Janko wore a false moustache, and hope that she had the wit and the resources to survive; it was one reason that she'd been chosen for this job.

And so—reluctantly—she moved away from the desk and began walking toward the entrance, wondering if she could somehow extract the Moroccan dagger from her bags, wondering just how she might preserve this life of hers that she was no longer sure of saving. As comfort she remembered that at least she'd been able to warn Youssef. What's more he had known exactly what she was talking about, which was more than she knew herself, and she marvelled at the impulse that led her to speak to him before she'd even learned that Ibrahim had met with trouble . . . as if, she thought, something deep inside of her had been picking up small clues all along the way, to be admitted to consciousness only when Janko had lost his moustache in her room.

Janko had warned her that he worked alone but there was more to it than that: something had gone horribly wrong without anyone knowing it, and there was no one to appeal to now, and no one to save her except herself.

6. *When* she hesitated a moment before climbing into the car Janko prodded her in the back with what he had described as a gun, and feeling the solidity and the weight of what pressed against her spine she saw little reason to doubt him. She slid into the front seat and when he joined her in the car it was impossible to overlook the fact that for the first time since they'd met he was not inquiring the name and address of the next informant. To quell the stricken feeling in the pit of her stomach she continued her masquerade of innocence, saying indignantly, "I resent very much your interrupting that phone call, it was my favorite scarf that was left behind at the cafe. I'm also hungry and I want breakfast and I also resent all this macho talk of a gun."

Pretend, she thought fiercely, *pretend that he doesn't guess your suspicions, forget knowing that he's finally—at last—going to demand the photos at gunpoint and when he learns they've been destroyed.* . . . Aloud she said coldly, "And now we drive to Tinehir, stopping en route for breakfast, I trust. May I see the map?"

"In the glove compartment."

This is pretending I will live to see Tinehir, she thought . . . *I will have to aim at his temple, the most vicious karate blow of all, used only when it's a matter of life or death and it's certainly going to come down to that . . . Once near him there are middle knuckle punches, slashes, snap kicks . . . I'm good at blocking . . . there's the wrist grab and the front choke and the back strangle . . . which? . . . and then the blow to the temple.*

But first she must find out who he was working for, and what was behind his betrayal. She must accuse, talk and learn, and hope to survive to expose him.

She busied herself unfurling the map and locating the Erfoud they were just leaving, and was startled to see how close they were to the Algerian border, separated from it by roughly a hundred miles of desert. Today they were heading north, she noted, returning to route 32, the highway down which they had driven yesterday and which wandered like a red necklace down the map through Tinehir, past a small town called El Kelaa—back in the mountains again—and then to Ourzazate, which was printed in very large letters. After Ourzazate a sharp turn to the south would take them again toward the desert and the Algerian border on their way to Zagora and then down to their last informant in Rouida. They were operating now inside the shape of a crescent, or a spacious alphabetic C.

C as in captive, she thought; *C as in catastrophe, as in cancel or calamitous,* and she folded up the map and put it away, determined to concentrate on the countryside. It had been too dark on their arrival last night to see the desert and they were surrounded now by signs of it; she was actually seeing palm trees, and gardens not yet planted but framed in squares of heaped-up earth to contain the scanty rainfall, and along the road were low barriers fashioned out of straw to hold back the sand that blew in from the desert to threaten the road. This was flat and tawny country, with only the occasional scattering of houses the same color as the pale sand, and always in the distance the mountains that hemmed in the land. It made a charming low-key melody of color and she tried to fix it in her mind as an antidote to her growing tension. A truck passed them, hauling wood, but cars were scarce again. They sped through a tiny village where three women in shapeless black garments and veils huddled in a doorway, looking very much like overgrown black crows, and barefooted children stood idly in the sand to watch them pass. As the sun moved higher the distant mountains turned rose-pink and the sand began to darken from pale beige to a harsh and pebbly yellow-brown.

Suddenly Janko slowed the car, braked and brought it to a stop. Turning her head to see what had caught his attention Mrs. Pollifax felt her heart constrict: the countryside that had struck her as empty was not entirely so, after all: two small dun-colored buildings occupied a rise in the ground, with a vaguely defined path leading up to them. The smaller of the two was a crumbling and roofless hut, its neighbor a solidly built and windowless structure crowned with a dome, a single palm tree shading it.

Janko backed the car and drove into the path leading up to the pair of them. She said lightly, "Are we sight-seeing?"

"It's a saint's tomb," he told her, and his voice was almost cheerful.

She sat very still, thinking, *A tomb, how very appropriate.*

"It's called a *koubba*," he added, "and you really ought to see one while you're here." There was excitement now in his voice and his eyes were shining with a kind of madness of anticipation that belied the calmness of his words so that she wondered if there would be time to learn about him at all.

He drove the car into the shade of the solitary palm and stopped the engine. Looking over the koubba she saw that it was sealed and inpenetrable, and she understood that it was the hut to which she'd be taken, with its empty shadowed doorway and crumbling square of window.

"Out," said Janko and now he produced the gun, a snub-nosed shiny M52 pistol.

"So it *is* a gun," she murmured, and looking him squarely in the eye, "Perhaps you plan to kill me here?"

He seemed taken aback by such directness. "Don't be absurd, I just want those photos," he told her. "Damn it, get out."

Her throat was dry and her heart beating fast but she was familiar with these symptoms, they were old friends by now and she knew their value; there were high costs to the heart in facing death many times but its imminence brought with it, as an act of kindness, the compensation of heightened awareness. She knew that she might die in the next hour but that she had been fortunate in living such a full life; she had also understood a long time ago that Carstairs' people did not always die in their beds. She opened the door and stepped out. Hearing the sound of a car on the road below she turned to look, but even if their presence was noticed she realized its driver would suppose they were only a pair of tourists examining a saint's tomb. Watching the small green car speed out of sight down the empty road she lifted her gaze for a last glance at the distant mountains, pale mauve in the sunlight, and then with Janko's gun at her back, and praying that he wouldn't shoot her from behind, she stepped over the rubble in the doorway and entered the hut.

The roof had long since collapsed but the rafters remained in place so that sunlight fell in stripes across the litter on the earthen floor. She found the hut larger than it had appeared from the road, with a matching window at the opposite end, and she brightened at this discovery: there was room for some maneuvering here after all . . . if she kept her wits about her . . . if he didn't shoot her first, before demanding the photos she no longer carried on her person. She picked her way across the room, stumbling a little over bricks, and looked for a space where the floor was clear of rubble. She found it not far from the rear window; only then did she turn to face Janko.

His glance was embracing the room, measuring its size and

possibilities, too; his gaze returned to her and he said flatly, "You will give me the photos now."

He stood at least ten feet away from her—too far—and she knew she had to think of a way to close the distance between them so that every blow, block and counter blow could be let loose in one great *jiyu kumite,* for she yearned to see him surprised, overcome, his arrogance humbled, plans smashed, his body dealt a blow to the floor. She was surprised by the vehemence of this longing but the problem lay in how to approach him until she remembered that she still wore Cyrus' money-belt around her waist, empty as it was now.

"Yes, of course the photos," she said, and began to loosen the waist of her khaki slacks. She reached under her shirt and detached the money-belt, her gaze fixed on Janko in case he might choose to kill her now that she was revealing their hiding place. Extracting the belt she walked toward Janko, holding it out to him.

He suspected nothing. As she came to a stop in front of him he reached out a hand for the belt and just before he grasped it she dropped it to the ground with a gasp of "oh—sorry!"

Automatically he bent to pick it up, and with her right hand she aimed a side hammerblow at his temple.

But she had miscalculated. He had moved so swiftly that as he retrieved the belt and straightened up the blow missed his temple and struck the side of his head, sending him sprawling flat across the rubble but still fully conscious and only a little dazed, the gun firmly in his hand and pointed at her. "You bitch!" he shouted, and lifted his gun.

She said quickly, "The photographs aren't in the money-belt."

"Not in the—Move! Get back," he shouted, stumbling to his feet, waving the gun at her with one hand and with the other fumbling at the pockets of the money-belt. *"Back!"* he shouted again and to emphasize his command he pulled the trigger and she felt the *swhish* of a bullet over her head.

She took a few steps to one side but she had no intention of moving back toward the window behind her. She was planning her next move, preparing herself for a high stamping kick with the heel of her foot, a strike aimed at the groin that could yet save her life, except that he would be wary now that he knew she was not defenseless, and she must be quick. His eyes remained fixed upon her as he began clumsily zipping open the pockets in the money-belt, one after another, and as he found each of them empty he waved his gun more wildly.

"Where?" he shouted, eyes livid. *"Where are the photos?"*

"I'll show you," she told him, taking a step toward him and concentrating mind, body and cunning on a leap to destroy him. But Janko's gaze had moved past her to the window behind her and she saw a look of utter bewilderment sweep across his face.

"No!" he gasped, and then he screamed, "No! It's not possible, you're dead!"

"Yisadda—believe," said a voice behind Mrs. Pollifax, and she spun around in astonishment.

⊙

7. *A* man stood framed in the window and what was even more astonishing than his presence was the fact that she recognized him because not so long ago they had met in a small shop in Er-Rachidia and he had helped her buy a Koran box: it was The Man With The Blue Eyes. Now he stood outside with a gun in his hand, and lifting it he fired twice; Janko fell to the ground,

gasped once, and was still. Climbing over the sill he walked past Mrs. Pollifax and knelt beside Janko to examine him.

"He's dead," he said.

"D-d-dead," she repeated, and abruptly sank down on the rubble-strewn floor.

"Totally, yes." He nodded grimly. "I don't usually go around shooting people but this s.o.b. did his best to kill me a few days ago and I've no interest in seeing him try again." With a narrowed glance at her he added, "You all right? Not in shock or anything?"

She said fervently, "On the contrary I'm terribly grateful to you—you seem to have just saved my life, but how—who—"

"Your karate's damn good," he told her. "I'd have shot him earlier but you kept getting in the way. Black belt or brown?"

"You've been outside all the time?" she gasped, and pulling her thoughts together she remembered what she'd seen just before entering the hut. In a surprised voice she said, "Do you happen to drive a small green car?"

"Very observant of you." He rose to his feet and she watched him carefully wrap his turban more closely around his tanned face with its thin black moustache and blue eyes. "But— who on earth are you?" she stammered. "He said you were dead and he believed it."

"Never mind that, let's get out of here," he told her. "Whether you realize it or not the police have been keeping track of you all day."

"Police?" she faltered. "But why the police? I thought—"

"*He's* police," he said, pointing to the dead man.

"*Janko?*"

He smiled. "Sorry but I'm Janko." He held out his hand and pulled her to her feet, saying abruptly, "I left my car several hundred yards down the road between two huge boulders." Leading her to the door he pointed. "See them? Climb into it

68

while I hide his blue Renault behind the koubba. It'll be found soon enough, but—what color's your luggage?"

Rallying, she said crisply, "One khaki bag, one blue, both canvas, and two djellabahs wrapped in newspaper." There would be time enough for explanations later, she told herself, and as she stumbled over the rubble past the threshold she glanced back into the dim room from which she was emerging with her life. This new and second Janko was going through the pockets of the first Janko, bringing out wallet, papers and at last the keys to the blue Renault. *I seem to be collecting Jankos,* she thought, and admitted to a certain dazed condition following the events of the past half hour. But *not* shock, she insisted firmly, unless it was a shock to be alive and to have collected another miracle. Nevertheless she found it a little difficult to plunge back into the reality in which she'd been living before she entered the hut; it needed the warmth of the sun on her face as she walked down the hill, and the intense blueness of the sky arching overhead to exorcise the nightmare of those past thirty minutes.

Now there was another Janko to think about, and work still to be done.

The car was a Peugeot, and had been well hidden. She climbed inside and sat staring into the seams of the two rocks while she disassembled all of her previous assumptions and tried to arrange them into a different pattern. She could admit to certain possible changes that pleased her but her mind still felt jarred. Aware of this new Janko opening the trunk of the car and slamming it closed she stilled her busy thoughts and waited, but when he joined her in the car she had reached one small decision. Saying "One moment, please," she leaned over, placed a hand on his moustache, dug in her fingers at one end and tugged hard.

"Ouch!" he gasped. "Damn it, that hurt, have you gone mad?"

"*His* moustache fell off—I had to be sure," she told him.

The new Janko laughed. "So that's what happened . . . Mine is a very small and pathetic moustache now. Obviously he felt obliged to wear one because I'm famous for my eyebrows and moustache—or was," he added, "and damn it I've resented very much sacrificing them, but I trimmed both of them on the plane here from Cairo. It was the only disguise I could manage, and not much of one at that." He backed the Peugeot out from the rocks and as they sped away from the saint's tomb and down the empty highway he gave her a quick shrewd glance. "When I searched him—he didn't get what he wanted from you, did he." It was a statement, not a question.

"No."

"You wouldn't be alive if he did." Carefully he asked, "What did he want from you?"

She realized that each of them had begun fencing now, not quite sure of the other yet; she said cautiously, "He was after certain photographs."

"Photos," he said deliberately, "of seven informants, one of whom may not match his photo and be an imposter?"

"Yes but he knew that much, too," she reminded him.

He nodded. "Right . . . Okay, you've had a difficult few days and too many Jankos, I understand that. You need some proof? How about the name Fadwa Ali?" When she shook her head, "Um al Nil?"

She was beginning to feel alarmed. "No to both—who *are* you?"

"How about the name Carstairs?"

She expelled her breath in a release of tension. "All right, Carstairs yes."

"Good. Then maybe you can trust me a little now. I've been

following you since Fez in a black car, and since Erfoud in this green one. I'm Maximillian Janko but my friends call me Max and I hope you will, too."

"Max," she repeated. "And I'm Emily Pollifax. But the other, the first Janko?"

He said in a hard voice, "He was my secretary in Cairo and his name is—was—Flavien Bernard, except it's obvious that he was a double agent all the time, which makes even that name suspect."

"Flavien Bernard," she said, frowning. "But how did he learn about this assignment to identify these seven people?"

"Oh very cleverly," said Max bitterly. "He was very frank about it before all hell broke loose, very proud of himself when he felt he'd nothing to lose by bragging. It seems he intercepted the initial request from Carstairs for an Arabic-speaking agent to travel in Morocco, extracted my documents and my resumé from the file, had his own photograph appended to them—after adding moustache and changing his eyebrows to roughly match my appearance—and wired it all to Langley, Virginia. When detailed instructions from Virginia were sent back he intercepted those, too, except that by the sheerest luck I stumbled across a copy of those just before he was about to leave, and confronted him with it."

"And how did he deal with that?" she asked.

He said in a savage voice, "By throwing me down an empty elevator shaft in Cairo after which he assumed, quite reasonably, that I was dead."

"Good God," she gasped, and remembering the strange reaction of Janko to the face in the window she understood his shock at seeing a man he'd believed dead. "Yet it didn't kill you," she marvelled, "because here you are."

He nodded. "I was lucky. I hate to even remember what

happened—" He shivered. "But he gave me such a push that I flew out and down—"

"Don't," she begged, seeing the expression on his face.

"No it's all right," he said with a twisted smile. "It may help the nightmares to talk about it. Of course it should have been curtains for me but he'd given me such a push that I was propelled away from the center of the shaft and along the outer wall. Two stories down I hit a beam, managed to grab it and hang there for longer than I care to remember, until finally I was able to pull myself up and lie across the beam. I was there for two ghastly hours, ten stories above the basement, before workmen came back from a damnably long lunch and heard my shouts."

She said soberly, "You were *very* lucky."

"By that time," he went on, "Flavien must have been already on a plane for Casablanca and then Fez. I took time only to sound a general alarm and to have my ribs taped—two of them got cracked when I hit that beam—and then I chartered a plane to fly me directly to Fez. All I knew was that at the last minute a Mrs. Pollifax had been assigned to join me—" He gave her the flash of a wry smile and added, "It certainly entertained me all the way to Fez as to what Flavien would think of *that*—but of course it also put you in very real danger. I was told that you'd both be found that first night at the Palais Jamai, and that's where I spotted the two of you in the bar late that afternoon—"

She nodded . . . when she had stopped for a brandy to steady her nerves and to tell him of Hamid ou Azu's murder in the souk.

"—and have been on your trail ever since."

She smiled. "Explaining Koran boxes to me in Er-Rachidia."

"Yes, I wanted to know what you were like," he admitted. "I had a fair idea of his plans for you and I wanted to get your measure." With an amused glance at her he said, "I decided you might be tougher than you looked, under that innocent facade, and that it would take a lot to scare you. I hoped so, anyway."

"Nevertheless he had begun to alarm me very much," she conceded. "But who was Janko—or Flavien—working for?"

He glanced into the rearview mirror and then at his watch. "There's not a car on the road, so nobody's following us, obviously, and do you realize I don't know where we head next? I think we've put enough distance behind us. There's a thermos of coffee in the back and I feel we could both use some. Shall we stop?"

"I appreciate your asking," she told him. "With coffee I just may survive this morning."

He drew off the road and they climbed out, finding themselves now on a vast plain of dull yellow sand and gravel that stretched flat for a great distance until it met with low, dun-colored mountains that exactly matched the earth. But the sun was shining and the sky was a vivid cloudless blue, and curls of steam rose from the coffee when he poured it into a cup and handed it to her.

"Bliss," she told him, smiling. "No breakfast."

He lifted his cup, looking grave. "A toast to the two of us, and a successful mission ahead."

"I'll drink to that," and as her first profession of faith she told him, "we head for Tinehir and informant number four, a man who sells fossils named Omar Mahbuba, and I ask again, who was the other Janko—this Flavien—working for?"

And standing there on the great sweep of flat and pebbly desert, empty except for telephone poles marching across its space, he told her.

"For Moroccan Intelligence."

"*Moroccan?*" she gasped. The knowledge stunned her; she had assumed many possibilities but not that he belonged to this country and that all the time he had possessed a network entirely his own here. Now she could understand why he'd sat calmly in a bar at the Palais Jamai while Hamid ou Azu was being murdered. He needed only to have picked up a phone as he entered the hotel; it would have taken only a minute, she could even picture him, receiver in hand, saying curtly, "The man is Hamid ou Azu, he can be found in the Fès el Bali selling brass-work. He is there now. *Go.*"

She stammered, "But I had assumed the informants—"

He shook his head. "All seven informants are Polisarios, every one of them . . . the nomad people, Saharans, fighting in the desert for their land, which used to be Western Sahara until Morocco moved in to occupy it."

Her instant and passionate reaction surprised her, and certainly it startled Max Janko. "I'm so relieved—"

"Relieved?"

"I had to come on trust," she explained earnestly. "Oh, I'm so glad I did. Because when Bishop told me, oh so sketchily about this war, I refused the assignment at first, my sympathies entirely with the—" She stopped and frowned. "But I was also told the United States gives support and weapons and money to Morocco *against* the Polisarios."

He said cautiously, "You have to understand that the CIA's not all of one piece, it has departments and sub-departments . . . In the mid-seventies Atlas was set up as a small unit entirely independent of the mainstream CIA." He stopped and then said abruptly, "Look here, didn't they tell you what you're up against, that this assignment is *Atlas?*"

She shook her head, puzzled. "Bishop only told me that very few people know about this department, that it's—separate, somehow."

"Separate!" he exploded. "You and I wouldn't have a leg to

stand on even if caught by bona fide CIA people here in Morocco, and they're here, I can assure you."

She said tartly, "Then it seems time for me to learn what you're talking about. What *is* Atlas?"

More calmly, he explained. "All right, this is how it happened. Back in the mid-seventies the CIA was found to be running some pretty cold-blooded covert operations and a good many scandals erupted. It was a bad time—I hear that your Congress very seriously considered outlawing CIA covert actions entirely."

"They've not exactly stopped," she put in dryly.

He ignored this. "Out of this grew Atlas, a small, very discreet group set up to research the precise opposite of the policies being pursued by any current administration so that if policies abruptly changed we'd be ready."

"How very intelligent," she commented. "Surprisingly so!"

He smiled appreciatively. "A little cynicism there? It's certainly intelligent in this particular case because now that Morocco and Algeria have established connections again, the United Nations just may be able to hold that plebiscite after all, the vote promised Western Sahara years ago. Damn late, of course, because Morocco's King has flooded Western Sahara with Moroccans in the meantime, but nevertheless it may happen at last." He smiled. "It should be added that in Washington there have always been doubts about this war between Morocco and the Polisarios. It's clearly understood—admitted publicly, too—that neither side can win, and that eventually there'll have to be negotiations and the Saharans will probably be given back at least some of their country.

"When that happens," he went on, "the question bothering a number of people is: to whom will the Polisarios turn once they achieve their Saharan Arab Democratic Republic? To Iran? to Libya? to the Soviet Union? Will they be open to friendship with the U.S., or remember instead that it was the U.S. who supported the King who claimed their land? We feel it vital to keep in touch—although I might add," he said dryly, "that in the greedy scheme of things this is not entirely philanthropy. Western Sahara also happens to have phosphate mines second only to Morocco's, which could lead to quite a cartel. Those mines are a vital key for the Saharans in that bleak desert country they fight for, it brings them added attention."

"But the Polisarios are Moslems? You mean Moslems are fighting Moslems in this war?"

He nodded.

"And strangest of all," she mused, "a network of Polisario informants running like a thread through Morocco!"

"And terribly, *terribly* dangerous for each of them," he said grimly. "In this country anyone sympathizing in the slightest degree with the Polisarios is clapped into prison at once. Amnesty International has been rather upset about this for some time, and about rumors of torture."

Torture, she thought with a shiver, remembering what had happened to her in Hong Kong. "Oh these small forgotten wars," she said angrily. There were questions still to ask. She didn't, for instance, see why on earth these Polisario informants would trust Atlas, given the circumstances, but as she felt the full impact of what he'd told her she glanced anxiously at the expanse of road behind them.

"But we shouldn't be stopping for so long," she said uneasily. "We'd better drive on now, surely? If the police are involved—if they've been watching, if they're looking for the blue Renault—they'll soon wonder where it is, won't they?"

He nodded. "A whole new ballgame now, yes. For you at least. When they find Flavien all hell will break loose, of course." He brought out a map and opened it. "Tinehir's only about a hundred miles away, and I think we're safe for a few

hours, but I don't think it sensible to enter Tinehir until dark."
He looked her over intently.

"What's the matter?"

"We don't match," he pointed out. "I'm in djellabah and
turban, and you're in tourist clothes." He began unwinding and
removing his turban, revealing a head of curly dark hair and
suddenly not looking like an Arab or Berber at all. "If we should
be stopped—they do sometimes stop cars looking for drugs,
I've been told—they'd recognize you. Have you a kerchief or
hat to cover your hair? At this point they don't know me or the
car—at least I don't think they do—but they've been seeing
you with Flavien ever since Fez, if only from a distance."

"Say no more," she said, and going to her two canvas bags
she delved into them to bring out a blue kerchief to tie around
her head, and a white shirt to replace the bright pink one she
wore. When she returned to Max he looked as Western as she
did, in slacks and shirt. "Are you American?" she asked.

He shook his head. "Actually I'm English, born in Zambia,
grew up in India, and went to college in America. Crazy,
what?"

She laughed. "I do believe I like you already."

Opening the car door for her he said, "It's all very well to
like me—I like you, too, by the way—but what about those
photos, do you trust me? Trust me enough to share them now?"

"I'm afraid you'll have to trust *me,*" she told him, and as
they resumed their drive she described her first two days with
the man he called Flavien; she told him of Hamid ou Azu's
murder, of waking in the night to find Flavien searching her
room, her learning of Ibrahim's arrest, her fears and suspicions
and the need she felt to destroy the photos. "The names and
addresses I can write down for you but unfortunately not the
photographs, and without them—"

He said soberly, "Without them they remain entirely in

your head." He nodded and said, "Obviously I'm going to have to guard you with my life, pamper and indulge you—"

"And feed me, too, I trust," she said with a twinkle.

He shook his head. "Flippancy aside, you do realize—however reluctantly—that this gives you a value that boggles the mind? How they'd love to find you!"

She gave him a startled glance. She supposed he was right but it had a certain jarring effect; she had not realized until now that she was the only person in the country who knew the appearance of the remaining informants, and this was information that the authorities of this country wanted very much. She was also the only person who could identify an imposter, which made her even more dangerous.

⊚

8. *Carstairs* was at his desk studying a memo when Bishop buzzed him on the intercom to say cheerfully, "Cairo's on line 3, sir, Fadwa Ali calling."

Carstairs frowned but not at the interruption; he frowned because communication among members of the Atlas group was kept rigidly minimal and this suggested trouble. "Scramble this call and come in, Bishop, I may need you." He picked up line 3 and said, "Carstairs here, how are you, Fadwa."

"Good morning yes," said Fadwa Ali. "You will scramble this please?"

"It's being done," Carstairs told him, and lifted an eyebrow at Bishop as he joined him.

"All taken care of," said Bishop, and sat down and picked up a phone to eavesdrop.

"There is trouble here," began Fadwa Ali, and Carstairs nodded. "We recommended to you most heartily a man by name of Max Janko, you are following me?"

"Yes," Carstairs said, his lips tightening. "And something's gone wrong?"

"Very," said Fadwa Ali. "The photo wired to you had been substituted by a double agent and was not that of Max Janko . . ."

Oh God, thought Carstairs, and said grimly, "Go on."

"Our man Janko had a secretary by name of Flavien Bernard. It is he who intercepted the request for an Arabic-speaking agent, all of which came through quickly, as you know, on an emergency basis and just before I left for Tunis. It is he who flew off to Morocco to meet your agent."

Carstairs drew in his breath sharply, his face turning into stone. Bishop, listening, thought *but our agent is Mrs. Pollifax, he means Emily . . .*

"You mean Mrs. Pollifax," Carstairs said, echoing Bishop's thought and only his face betraying his shock.

Fadwa said, "We've still not uncovered Flavien's real identity—fabricated, obviously, despite every security check, but what matters, of course—"

Carstairs swore. "What matters is that my agent Mrs. Pollifax would have turned over the names and photographs of all seven informants to him, which means death to seven people and probably for Mrs. Pollifax as well." He added bitterly, "He has also killed our man Janko, I assume?"

Fadwa broke in to say, "I felt it compulsive that you know the worst at once but there is still some hope."

"We could use that hope," Carstairs told him curtly.

"Already one miracle has occurred, our man survived what should have been a horrible death. He was thrown down an empty elevator shaft. We understand there was confrontation and Flavien arranged this, and since it occurred on the tenth floor, this Flavien—" he spat out the name, "assumed him dead, but Janko survived. A miracle, as I say. He clung to a beam on floor eight for two hours and was rescued by workmen. He called the office from the airport moments before flying off to Fez to look for Flavien. Not in good shape, you understand, but alive."

Carstairs whistled. "Good man! And then?"

Fadwa sighed. "There ends the miracle. I delayed my call, expecting to hear from Janko once he reached Fez. I have heard nothing."

"Not good."

"No. If you read his dossier you know he is very good in the office with the documents, the books, the languages, the codes, but not experienced in the fieldwork. He left with two cracked ribs, he said, and there must surely have been some shock. Worse, he left with no gun. He may have had trouble securing a gun in Fez, and without a gun he would have been a fool to confront this Flavien in the hotel, considering who the man must be. One can only hope he did not."

Carstairs sighed. "I understand."

"I can tell you this, however," continued Fadwa, "that in repeated calls to the Palais Jamai hotel in Fez we have learned that a Mr. Max Janko and a Mrs. Reed-Pollifax each checked out of the hotel at 5 A.M. yesterday."

"Five A.M.! At least she was still alive then," Carstairs said with some relief. "But if she left with the wrong Max Janko—if she left with this Flavien chap—then damn it, Fadwa, my agent has no idea she's traveling with the wrong man." He stopped as a more bitter thought overtook him.

It was Fadwa who expressed the thought. "Or she was disposed of once the hotel was left and is not traveling with him at all. One must prepare oneself . . . Once she turned over the list and the photos she would have been of no use to him at all."

Disposed of, thought Bishop, *he's speaking of Mrs. Pollifax, he's saying she may have been murdered, why does he use such a hideous phrase "disposed of" it sounds inhuman, he means dead, he means that she may be dead at this very minute, never understanding why or what we sent her into, and in another minute I'm going to be sick . . .*

Carstairs had drawn out a file and was saying, "We mustn't assume anything, Fadwa, we've got to do what we can and use that hope of yours. You weren't given the names of the informants, I'm going to give you the name of one of them now. Can you write this down?"

"Anything—just tell me." For the first time there was emotion in Fadwa Ali's voice and Bishop understood his stress, too.

"I'm going to give you the name of the informant in Fez and I want you to find out by hook or by crook—in this kind of emergency you have permission to break telephone silence, although God only knows if there are telephones in the medina —I want you to somehow find out whether informant number one in Fez is alive and well."

"Good. Give it to me."

"His name is Hamid ou Azu," he said, spelling it out, and he gave instructions as to where the souk could be found.

"I have it written," said Fadwa. "I have also a contact in that area who can visit this souk within the hour—very discreetly, you understand, no questions asked why. It will be carefully done, I assure you."

"Good—call me back the minute you hear."

"Of course. Any other names?"

Carstairs said quietly, "You know the need for secrecy, I'm risking a great deal sharing even this by telephone. Just find out if number one is safe. If not—"

"Yes?"

He said wearily, "If not, we're in even more trouble, we rethink the situation and begin again."

When he had hung up Bishop said savagely, "Damn."

Carstairs nodded. "My sentiments precisely but there's no point in giving up Mrs. Pollifax for dead until we have more information." He gave his assistant a rueful, twisted smile. "We've sat here a hell of a lot of times mourning her, Bishop, and somehow she's always made it."

"Not like this time," snarled Bishop. "You heard Fadwa Ali, we delivered her into the hands of a bastard who tosses people down elevator shafts. As soon as she turned over that list of names to him, and above all the photographs—*as we instructed her to do, damn it*—"

"Softly, softly," chided Carstairs.

"But there must be something we can do!"

Carstairs said quietly, "Yes, we can get back to work and wait to hear from Fadwa."

Bishop gave him a furious glance and strode toward the door to his office.

"Bishop."

Reluctantly he turned.

"You know as well as I do this is a dangerous business and that Mrs. Pollifax understands this."

"Does she?" Bishop said stiffly. "Maybe she did in the beginning but she's had such a run of success and luck I'll bet she's forgotten failure is also a possibility."

Carstairs patiently repeated, "There's nothing just now that any of us can *do*, Bishop."

"Except wait," he complained bitterly.

But it was not necessary for them to wait even the promised hour. Because the news was bad, Fadwa's return call was being scrambled only forty minutes later. There had been no need for his Fez contact to personally look for Hamid ou Azu. "Everyone in the medina knows he is dead," said Fadwa in a dreary voice. "He was murdered Sunday afternoon, in his souk, in the light of day. A knife in his back. No one knows who killed him, no one saw."

"I see, yes," said Carstairs, blinking. "Yes, that does change matters, doesn't it."

"I am without hope," said Fadwa. "He will have murdered your agent now, too."

With a glance at Bishop's stunned face Carstairs said smoothly, "The agent I sent is no fool, Fadwa, let us not give up hope yet."

"But you said she was—a *woman?*"

Carstairs smiled faintly, and with his eyes on Bishop he said firmly, "A woman who once led an escape party out of Albania with two wounded men in tow, and against all the odds in the book. There may not be many of us, Fadwa—and this may be the end for Atlas—but there is the seed of an idea growing in my mind. It needs some thinking."

"You said from *Albania?*" echoed Fadwa in disbelief.

"From Albania, yes."

"But what can be done now?"

"Give me some time, Fadwa, I'll get back to you soon."

When he put down the phone Bishop said suspiciously, "What 'seed of an idea'? Was that to cheer up Fadwa or me? There's no one to appeal to for help. You know how small the Atlas group is, you can't even take this to Upstairs because Mornajay's gone off on holiday."

Carstairs said lightly, "Yes, Mornajay is surprising, isn't he, this man who never took a vacation until that abrupt and mysterious trip he made to Thailand a year ago? And since then he's taken a week's holiday in July and has departed now for two weeks in January. Very healthy change, don't you think?"

Bishop gaped at him. "We're talking about Mornajay's health at a time like this?"

Carstairs smiled. "Shame on you, Bishop, you've forgotten where he's vacationing . . . He's in Spain, Bishop—Spain, just across the Strait of Gibraltar from Morocco. Call his secretary, will you, and find out where he can be reached today."

Bewildered, Bishop said, "But what can *he* possibly do?"

Carstairs sighed. "Bishop, until the tape runs out on this, until we hear otherwise, we'll proceed—we *must* proceed—as if Mrs. Pollifax is alive. In trouble perhaps but alive. If she survives we know where she'd be heading. We dare not wire photographs but we have the names of the villages on her list. We can send a man to the end of the line, to Zagora and to Rouida, in case she makes it through."

"You really think—but who?"

"Mornajay, of course," said Carstairs, and sat back comfortably in his chair. "Mornajay is CIA and he's also Atlas, and he's one of the Upstairs people, he's got clout and he has experience. Vacation or not, we need to know what's happening and he's the man to find out."

"Thank God," murmured Bishop, and leaned over the intercom, punched a double-digit number, reached Mornajay's secretary and handed the receiver to his superior.

A moment later Carstairs was saying, "Mrs. Hudson? Carstairs here, and can you tell me, please, how to reach Mornajay as quickly as possible, definitely today, preferably within the next hour, if not in the next five minutes?"

9 •

They had been driving in silence for some time, but it was a comfortable silence as each of them digested the events of the past hours. Mrs. Pollifax was full of questions but was ignoring them, she was still experiencing the surprise and the joy of being alive and this brought a flood of pleasurable sensations about her new companion and about the country through which they were passing. It was true they were driving through a bleak and stony wasteland that stretched flat as a carpet flung down between distant mountains. It was a schema limited to only two colors but those two colors were the sapphire blue of sky and mountains, and the rich terra-cotta of earth. Feeling admitted to life once more, not only in the largest sense but in the sense of being acknowledged by the man sitting next to her, a man who was open to response and communication, she postponed thinking for a little while of the odds against them and of their chances of evading the authorities. She was happy.

They were passing now a line of conical shapes in the sand, like small volcanoes interrupting the endlessly flat surface, and Max slowed the car to peer at them through the window. "I believe those are wells—maybe foggaras," he said. "Mind if I stop and dash over to look?"

"I'll dash with you," she told him. "But what are foggaras?"

"Ancient irrigation systems dating back centuries," he flung over his shoulder as he raced across the road to the small hills with their cone-shaped peaks. Climbing to the top of one he called down to her, "They're certainly wells, or used to be.

They're all choked with sand now. It was the slaves who did all the incredible digging to tap underground water and any number of them died of suffocation when the walls caved in on them."

Mrs. Pollifax climbed to the top of the one next to Max, looked down into its sand-filled crater and hastily drew back. Watching her he nodded. "Exactly. It could happen to you too if you fell in—like quicksand, I imagine."

He slid down to join her on solid ground and they stood a minute looking around them, at the incredibly blue sky and the expanse of stones and sand. "What a savagely beautiful country," she murmured, "and yet—why does it seem so dark in spite of the bright sun and sky?"

"Its history is dark, that's what you feel," he said. "Morocco is actually a country quite new to the modern world, it entered it just before the First World War and this particular part of it wasn't tamed for another three decades. At the beginning of this century—and well into it, as a matter of fact—there were neither maps nor roads in all of Morocco, only caravan trails." He stretched one arm toward the high and distant mountains to the east. "On the other side of those mountains the Sultans lived in sybaritic splendor—in Fez, Meknes, Rabat and Marrakech—but this part of the country was called the *bled-el-sida,* the lands of dissidence."

"They didn't like Sultans?"

He grinned. "Oh, they honored the Sultan as Commander of the Faith, they simply refused to pay taxes to him. The tribal chiefs built their castles and fortresses high up in the Atlas mountains and happily fought their blood feuds and wars of honor in their own ways. So occasionally a Sultan would make a procession over the mountains to collect the taxes personally. He would bring his wives, his concubines, slaves, ministers, armies and hundreds of tents and horses—can you imagine that?—and he'd meet with the tribal chiefs and demand their allegiance and their taxes."

"All the way from the north?" she said in astonishment. "From Fez or Rabat?"

He nodded. "All the way. Not often, obviously, since it took the better part of a year."

"And they would pay?"

"Not always willingly," he said. "From what I've read the Sultan would decapitate those who refused to pay, after which the heads would be salted and taken back to Fez to be hung on the gates of the palace."

Mrs. Pollifax shivered. "I hope that was a *very* long time ago."

He shrugged. "On the contrary, this side of the Atlas mountains wasn't tamed by the French until 1934—and I might add the French were no less cruel, seldom taking prisoners."

Puzzled she said, "But why did France want it?"

"Oh everyone wanted it," he said, "and that's what kept it from being conquered for so long. Morocco lies at the head of the Mediterranean, you see, only thirty miles away from Gibraltar, with Spain beyond it, but the French especially wanted it because they'd already taken over Tunisia and Algeria, and adding Morocco made a nice little basket of goodies." He shook his head. "The conquest of Morocco—and it took decades—was a bloody *bloody* one, full of treachery, betrayal and cruelties on both sides."

She said soberly, "That certainly explains what I've been feeling. I thought at first it was all the negatives that Janko emitted—or Flavien—but it's been lingering. You're much pleasanter to travel with, you know—he merely grunted."

Max smiled. "Perhaps my greatest charm is that I've no interest in killing you."

"That *is* important in a friendship," she told him gravely, with a twinkle in her eye, and they retraced their steps to the car.

As they set out again for Tinehir she said, "But you must explain to me why on earth any Polisarios would ever trust this Atlas group."

"That's easy," he told her. "I gather that it's due entirely to the Carstairs chap who sent you here. How well do you know him, did you know he began intelligence work in the OSS during World War II?"

"Yes I did," she said, smiling as she remembered how she'd learned of Carstairs' history during her second adventure. "He worked in Occupied France smuggling out people and information and his code name was Black Jack."

Max gave her a startled glance. "Good heavens, you know quite a lot about him, and certainly more than I do! But he didn't spend all the war years in France, you see. Later, as a sort of rest cure, he was sent to North Africa as a liaison officer, because of his fluent French, except it wasn't long before he was given charge of a commando raid on a Tripoli ammunition dump—I suppose because of his earlier experience in Europe."

"After becoming thoroughly rested, one hopes," she put in.

"Well yes, one does hope that," he said, "because it meant an endless trek across the desert in Land Rovers, and then sneaking unseen into a dark city occupied by the enemy. But that's where he worked with a mixed bag of Europeans and North Africans, one of them a Moroccan who saved his life."

Startled, she said, "My goodness, what happened?"

"As I understand it, they found the ammo dump and set the charges, the dump was due to blow up in seconds and they all raced away, except that Carstairs fell over an ammo crate and broke his leg. It was his Moroccan companion who came back for him, risking his own life to do it, and carried Carstairs out of Tripoli while all hell broke loose."

She said softly, "And if he hadn't gone back for him—"

"Exit Carstairs."

She nodded. "So he owes his Moroccan friend all the years of his life since then."

"Yes."

She thought of how knowing Carstairs had changed her own life, and of the work he'd done since then, and of the others whose lives he must have changed or saved, and she felt again that small shiver that occurred to her when events hinted at a destiny being played out, of unseen forces intervening. She said soberly, "It would certainly be a privilege to meet a man like that, who would risk his own life for a friend."

He gave her a quick glance. "It's possible that we may both meet him because I've a hunch he's one of the informants. It was this man whom Carstairs approached, of course, when he thought of setting up this particular network. They've kept in touch over the years, you see."

She was not surprised. "It would have to be like that, yes, for such trust to have been established." With a stab of anxiety she added, "I do hope he wasn't the Hamid ou Azu who was murdered in Fez."

"I hope so, too."

The mountains had begun moving in closer, sending out great tentacles of stone in the shape of flat-topped mesas. Trees were beginning to appear in the distance and soon they were passing a compound of adobe houses, with a cow tethered to the wall and a girl standing next to it wearing a long red skirt over bright pink pants and a green scarf around her head. The desert had receded, to be replaced by fields that grew increasingly lush and green.

"Grain for couscous," Max said. "I think we must be nearing Goulmima, halfway to Tinehir."

"Does that mean food?" asked Mrs. Pollifax wistfully. "I'm so *very* hungry."

"I know you are," he said, "and I'll risk looking for some edibles but I think you stay in the car and hide under the blanket in the back. You've got to keep in mind that you may already be of great interest to the police."

"Do you think they've found Flavien's body yet? It's only been what, a few hours?"

"Intelligence agents and police can do a hell of a lot if they're worried enough. My guess is that it's too early and they haven't found him yet but we mustn't count on it." He added soberly, "But it's not just that . . . When I followed you out of Er-Rachidia you were trailed only a short way by the police. You remember the military compound we passed before we stopped for coffee?"

She winced. "I didn't notice."

"Understandable," he said, "it looked like any other adobe compound except for the insignia on the gate. My guess is that an arrangement was set up to keep track of your progress without actually tailing you in a car, which would certainly be conspicuous in this sort of pre-desert country. I think once your departure was established you were only followed for a few miles and then a phone call was made to the next military headquarters and a lookout posted."

"In which case the blue Renault has not been seen by the next lookout."

"Exactly. So whether Flavien's body has been found or not is academic for the moment. He's mysteriously disappeared somewhere between Erfoud and Goulmima.

"What's worse," he added gloomily, "there wasn't time for me to collect a fake passport so I entered the country under my own name and it won't take them long to discover there's a real Max Janko in Morocco. They'll start tracing the cars I rented and find that I've been following the two of you, and then they'll begin setting up roadblocks to corner us."

She sighed. "*Not* a happy situation, no."

"Happy! It scares the hell out of me. We can't possibly expect to drive this car the length of the country without being caught."

She nodded. "Then we'll have to abandon the car, we've no other choice."

"But then what? My God, then what?"

She said calmly, firmly, "I think we simply *must* risk Tinehir, but after that we'd be fools to keep this car. We'll have to abandon our luggage, too, of course."

"Damn it you're right—and *nobody* to turn to for help," he added savagely.

"That's not true," she told him quietly. "There are the Polisario informants we were sent to find."

Max's laugh was bitter. "If we can find them."

"In Tinehir there's Omar Mahbuba."

"Sure—unless he's the imposter we were sent to locate, and if so, God help us, we'll have no chance at all."

She looked at him curiously. "How very pessimistic you are suddenly! There are *always* chances."

He said hotly, "I like your faith but I don't share it."

"Perhaps you're not as experienced as I am? If one becomes desperate enough—"

He laughed. "Experienced! You didn't know? This is my first real job in the field. Languages and statistics and translations are my specialty, I work in an office, and they only chose me because I speak Arabic."

"Oh," said Mrs. Pollifax, taken aback, and realized that her reaction to this was a feeling of doubled responsibility that made her feel rather tired. On the other hand, when she thought about his confession more reasonably, she rallied almost at once: her companion might not be experienced but he had already managed to abort two murders, his own and hers. "No one would ever realize that you're inexperienced," she told him, and was able to say it with complete sincerity; she also felt it time to return to her original objective. "About that food, about lunch—?"

He laughed. "Right you are . . . tenacious, too." Bringing the car to a stop beside the road he reached over and opened the door for her. "Into the back with you to hide, we're nearly in Goulmima."

She was not to see Goulmima but Max very kindly kept up a running commentary for her. "Much brighter town," he called over his shoulder. "Very charming iron grillwork over the windows, and I just saw two women scurrying into an alley and neither of them wore black—amazing—and—ah, I see a *baehl*, a food store. I'll park around the corner from it." He braked and turned off the ignition. "I'm leaving now and locking the doors," he told her. "Not suffocating or anything are you?"

"No."

"Good."

She heard his footsteps fade away, leaving her to thoughts that she would have preferred not to entertain, such as what on earth they would do without a car once they abandoned it in Tinehir. In Fez Hamid ou Azu was dead, in Er-Rachidia Ibrahim had been arrested, in Erfoud she had been able to warn Youssef but they still had to reach Tinehir, then Ourzazate, Zagora and —at the very edge of the desert—the village of Rouida, and if they succeeded in reaching the latter, what then? Trapped!

Stop, she told herself fiercely, *you're hungry, that's all, Emily*. She turned her thoughts to counting the hours since she'd had food, and had just reached eighteen when she heard Max's voice again.

"Yes yes, *Ingileezeeya*," he was saying. "Now go away, no more basheesh, comprenez-vous? Scram! Nice meeting you but go." Shrill children's voices rose in a clamor as he opened the door and took the wheel. A moment later the engine came to life and the voices died away as the car was set in motion. Over his shoulder he said, "I hate seeing children beg and they cost me nine dirhams, blast it. You can come up for air in a few minutes, we're only fifty miles from Tinehir now."

From the sound of his voice she guessed that he, too, had spent some of the past fifteen minutes in reflection and that his thoughts had been equally as troubled as hers. But he had returned with half a dozen oranges, four tins of sardines and two bottles of mineral water; her unwelcome fast was ending.

IO. *Tinehir* was a hill village, all cream and terra-cotta in the late afternoon sun. They had decided to risk one brief foray into the town in daylight, because—as Mrs. Pollifax had pointed out—if they waited until dark they would have to ask directions and they might be remembered if the police followed them to Tinehir. There were also several hotels but Omar Mahbuba and his fossil shop could only be found near one of them.

Allowing themselves one discreet inquiry of a ragged-looking old man, they learned that the hotel they wanted stood on the tall hill overlooking the town, and the winding road to it branched off from the main street. With this established they headed immediately out of town to spend the next two hours waiting for the sun to slip behind the mountains. With their car hidden behind a treeless hill they began to regretfully but ruthlessly empty their suitcases and bags of all but the few essentials that would fit into one knapsack and Mrs. Pollifax's large purse.

"Everything is image in this area," Max told her, scowling darkly. "A lady tourist does not carry a suitcase but a male tourist may wear a knapsack."

"I refuse to give up my djellabahs," she warned him.

"Oh, *definitely* we hang onto the djellabahs, we may need them if we grow conspicuous, but—" Looking her over critically, "You could certainly carry *them*—wrapped in newspaper, of course—without destroying your Tourist Image. You could have just bought them."

Heartened by this, Mrs. Pollifax returned to the process of selection. She chose her heaviest sweater to wear under her trench coat; for Max's knapsack she handed over a change of shirt and socks, toothbrush, hairbrush and comb, her jars of vitamin tablets and aspirin. Traveler's checks, money and passport remained in her purse and she found space there for her collapsible drinking cup, water-purifying tablets, the guidebook and the Moroccan dagger.

Max added the turban from his earlier disguise, and his *choukhara*—the flat leather over-the-shoulder bag that natives wore with djellabahs—their maps, a change of socks, two packets of dried soup and a wool cap.

Now as they drove back into Tinehir at dusk they looked for a small side street not too far from the hotel in which to abandon the Peugeot.

"I think it would be very kind," said Mrs. Pollifax, "to leave the car key in the lock of the trunk so that all its contents can be stolen *quickly*. I mean, I'd much rather someone in need use them and not the police."

"I'll buy that," said Max, and edged the car between two

wretched-looking and dilapidated adobe houses and killed the engine. "Out—fast," he ordered.

She quickly slid out, Max locked the doors of the car and left the key inserted in the lock of the trunk. Carrying knapsack and bundle they slipped into the shadows, two tourists strolling toward the road leading up the hill to the hotel.

Some fifteen minutes later they reached the summit, panting a little from the ascent and discovering that while they had plodded doggedly up the steep hill the sky had darkened and was illuminated by stars and a rising half-moon. They stood a moment on the parapet looking out over the city at shadowed squares of adobe houses and at the starkly silhouetted sweep of mountains beyond the city. Behind them stood the hotel, flat-roofed, sprawling and luxurious, but when they strolled closer they could see no cluster of shops: the hotel occupied the entire crest of the hill. As they stood in the shadows, staring wistfully at the bright lights of the hotel, a car roared up the hill, turned and came to a stop at the entrance. Two men stepped out, and as they reached the circle of light spilling from the lobby Max drew her deeper into the shadows.

"Stay back, I don't like the look of them," he whispered.

"Why?" she whispered back.

"Plainclothesmen look the same all over the world," he told her grimly. "Same black suits, same gray serious faces."

"Looking for us—or for me, do you think?"

He didn't reply. "Let's search for that fossil shop of yours. If it's supposed to be near the hotel then it's damned well got to be somewhere around here. C'mon, there's a paved walkway leading around the hotel, let's see what's on the other side."

Ten minutes later they found it: the tiny shop was set just below the hotel on a dirt lane that was lined with other narrow adobe buildings. Words printed on a sign read FOSILS—SUVENIRS. A solitary light bulb hung suspended above three wooden steps leading up to a shabby porch where a door stood open, show-ing a well-lighted area beyond. A gypsy-looking girl of eleven or twelve squatted on the top step rinsing small glass cups in a shallow pan of water; she wore a purple flowered skirt over bright red pants, a blue shirt and torn sneakers. When she smiled shyly at them her teeth were brilliant against her dark skin. Putting aside her cup-washing she ran ahead of them into the shop, calling out to someone unseen, and vanished through a doorway festooned with strings of beads.

They walked inside, finding the tiny room on their right empty of people but filled with objects. "Not just fossils," murmured Mrs. Pollifax, looking around the room at walls hung with carpets and knives, row upon row of fossils and gleaming stones, a gorgeous brass and copper brazier, and wicker baskets filled with beads and necklaces of polished stone. A faded photograph of the King hung on the wall.

A voice from the tiny room on their left quickly distracted her, and she turned: a pair of tourists, man and woman, stood examining a large brass kettle. The proprietor of the shop waited patiently beside them. Now he turned to look at Mrs. Pollifax and Max, a raffish-looking man with sharp eyes and a stubble of beard, short and wearing a shabby brown djellabah.

Beside her Max said anxiously, "Well?"

She nodded. "The right shop and the right man. He matches his photo, Max—he's Omar."

"Thank God," said Max fervently.

The beaded curtains parted again, and the girl came out carrying a tray with two glasses of mint tea for them. When they thanked her she did not smile but returned at once to the porch to continue washing glasses in the pan of water. Leaving the tourists to continue their discussion about the brass kettle Omar Mahbuba came to them with a polite smile. "I show you beautiful objects?"

Max nudged Mrs. Pollifax. Not knowing just how to approach him she said, "Hamid ou Azu is dead."

He looked at her blankly. "A fine carpet? Many fossils, many stones? Come see."

Max said uneasily, "I think he went genuinely blank, you're sure this is the right man?"

Trying again Mrs. Pollifax said flatly, "You are Omar Mahbuba."

Startled, he looked at her, puzzled, frowning, and reluctantly nodded.

She said, "There is in Erfoud a young man named Youssef Sa—"

"*Yuaf!* Stop!" he cried sharply, and he called out words to the girl on the steps. When she hurried in he pointed to the tourists, went quickly to the beaded doorway and gestured Max and Mrs. Pollifax to follow him.

It was another tiny room, holding a rug, a pillow, a radio and an Arabic calendar on the wall, no more. Once inside he turned on them fiercely. "What is this? Who are you?"

She turned to Max. "You take over, you speak Arabic."

"I talk some English," the man said. "Speak!"

Mrs. Pollifax said, "In Fez there was Hamid ou Azu—he has been killed with a knife, a *khanjar*," she told him. "In Er-Rachidia there is a waiter named Ibrahim who has been arrested by the police."

He looked puzzled and wary. "But Youssef?"

"There was time to warn him, I think he's safe. Now we warn you—there is trouble, something is wrong."

He looked at them, frowning. "You are Christians, you are *nasrani* . . . American? English? How is it you know such things? Should I kill you or believe?"

Max said dryly, "I earnestly beg you to believe."

"Tell him what's happened," she said, "and do explain to

him the trouble we're in now, too. Deep trouble." She sat down on a pile of folded rugs, tired from the long steep hill, from the day's suspense and from nearly being murdered as well.

Searching for words Max began explaining in Arabic. She caught only the words *photographs, police* and *moustache,* the rest being unintelligible. Apparently Max's storytelling was not mesmeric because Omar interrupted him to say impatiently, "Show me the pictures then!"

Max began again, this time explaining the lack of photographs—she did not envy him—and she had to laugh when Omar placed his hands over his ears and said in English, "Stop! This is a tale from Harun al-Rashid! What can I do but believe?" In a craftier voice, very low, he added, "I will trust you more if you tell me this: where do you go next to warn of this?"

Mrs. Pollifax answered. "To Ourzazate, to a certain barber."

A smile spread slowly over his face, broadening to show a missing tooth; he nodded, pleased. "We have a proverb, Trust in Allah but tether your camel first . . . I believe now."

Max shook his head. "I hope we don't have to go through all this in Ourzazate—if we ever get there."

Omar said absently, "No no, there are words I can give you to say to him." He frowned. "This Hamid you spoke of, and this Ibrahim I do not know, but I know the name of the one who passes certain—shall we say merchandise—to me, and the one I send it to. Beyond this, no. You think Youssef is safe? Were you followed here to me?"

Max leaped in to explain the car abandoned in an alley below, and their hope that Omar might hide them for the night and help them on their way to Ourzazate. "If you plan to leave maybe we could leave together—"

Mrs. Pollifax shook her head. "That would be dangerous for him, Max."

"Yes I suppose so," he said regretfully. "Then if you could

somehow think of a way to get us out of here, a different car or even donkeys?"

"Donkeys! You?" He laughed. "I need to think, I need time. For me it is better for Nadija and me—she is my daughter—to go south, disappear into the *bled,* the country. I have a cousin—"

His daughter was calling to him. "Wait here," he said. "My two customers buy."

Max joined her on the rug. "I suppose he sleeps on this, it's his bed?"

"Quite possibly. Tired?"

"Worried is more like it. I hate depending on Omar for help."

She said dryly, "Not too long ago you worried there would be no help at all . . . If that man has lived a double life for more than a dozen years, Max, then I imagine he's cleverer than either of us."

Omar returned, stuffing coins and bills into some inner repository among the folds of his djellabah. "We have busy night, I think. To help you yes, but also for me to be gone by morning."

Max said in surprise, "You can leave that fast?"

Regarding him curiously Mrs. Pollifax said, "Will you be sad at leaving here?"

He shrugged. "My sons already are fighting in the desert. Since my wife died I have been eager to join them, but—" Proudly, "I most helped my brothers in the desert by staying here." He gestured toward his shop. "Always I am ready to pack and go," he confided. "You see how small my souk. You have eaten?"

They each shook their head.

Rummaging in a bag he handed Max a slab of goat cheese.

"Eat while we think. It is important you go to Ourzazate—and beyond," he said significantly, "so we must think hard."

Mrs. Pollifax nodded, and clinging to one of her three Arabic words, as well as to her portion of the cheese, she said *"Shukren."*

"We have money," Max told him.

"How much?"

Max brought out Moroccan bills and Mrs. Pollifax added her own to them.

"Good," Omar said, nodding. "Very good. I am thinking of Mustapha Benhima's wish to sell his old truck. I can ask what dirhams he wants for it, I can tell him I owe a *fabor* to a friend in El Kelaa who looks for an old truck."

"But how long will that take? We have only the night," Max said nervously.

Very gently Omar reproved him. "I too must hurry but if patience is bitter it bears a sweet fruit. We are all in the hands of Allah—rest while I do what I must do."

"You could let us help," suggested Mrs. Pollifax.

"Not rest?"

"How can one rest at such a time?"

He nodded. "True. That is so. Very well, you can help Nadija roll up rugs in the souk while I go to see Mustapha. In the night I must load my own truck when no one will see me. Later we will eat."

Surprised, Mrs. Pollifax said, "You take only the rugs?"

He smiled. "The rugs are my wealth, the jewelry and the brass. Fossils and beads?" He spat. "They are for tourists who buy anything, but with my rugs—where I go, which is to the desert—my rugs can be traded for many things. A camel. Goats. Sheep. A tent. Food. Guns."

With this he vanished like a shadow out into the darkness.

There were eight rugs, and beautiful ones: Berber rugs,

Tuareg rugs, Moroccan rugs—Mrs. Pollifax marvelled at them but they were heavy to detach from the walls and it was strenuous work. Rolling them up as tightly as possible Nadija brought cord to secure them and they piled them next to the door, which was closed and locked now. From a corner Nadija, the practical one, brought several clay pots and a huge brass charcoal brazier. These she lovingly added to the growing pile, and then she brought out goat cheese, a loaf of bread and from somewhere produced two cans of cola. They picnicked atop the pile of rugs, and once in a while Nadija gave them a quick shy smile. Mrs. Pollifax saw that she had packed small things of her own in a greasy leather bag tied with string: a comb, earrings, a few coins, a small copy of the Koran and silver bracelets.

It was already ten o'clock, a long two hours, when Omar returned and dropped keys into Max's lap. "You have a truck," he said. "An old Volvo, very old, but it drives . . . He bargained hard for it and has gone to bed now I *think*, but still, he is a little—" He made a face.

"Suspicious?" asked Max sharply.

Omar nodded. "*Temān* . . . before dawn we must be gone."

"How about gas?"

"That was hardest part of bargain but it has petrol, yes, and a tin of extra. My own truck is in back. Nadija—" He spoke to her in Arabic and she nodded, picking up the smaller bundles while Omar shouldered a rug.

Max leaped up to help and presently Mrs. Pollifax rose with a sigh to join them, thought better of it, lay down on the rug and at once fell asleep.

When she opened her eyes it was to find Omar and Max standing over her, both looking amused. She sat up and saw that both rooms were stripped down to their bare and flaking walls and the little shop was empty except for a few remaining baskets of stones and beads. A glance at her watch told her that it was 3 A.M. but her several hours of sleep had refreshed and changed her, and she sprang to her feet.

"It's time to go," Max told her. "The town's asleep and Omar's truck is packed, he suggests we leave before he does, and he's given directions."

She nodded. "All right, we leave first. What sort of truck have we?"

He shrugged. "The tires are thin and worn but the engine seems okay." He added pointedly, "Omar thinks that by morning there may be police looking for two American tourists about whom there is much curiosity because they've been missing since Erfoud . . . Nadija heard this when she went to draw water at the well. So as long as we are here, in Omar's souk—"

"—he's in danger. Say no more."

"Right." He suddenly smiled. "And now, my dear Mrs. P., it's time for that djellabah, and a veil, and for you to become a native. Tourists do not ride in battered old trucks."

With interest she donned the robe, finding it as comfortable as a bathrobe over her sweater and slacks. She then gave her full attention to Omar, who showed both of them how to wind the veil around her head so that it covered all but her eyes.

"Nadija—?"

The girl opened her leather bag, brought out a wooden vial and a stick, and applied kohl to Mrs. Pollifax's eyebrows, turning them thick and dark.

"Voila! Very very good," said Max, grinning. "Can you give her a name, Omar?"

"Aisha?"

She had become Aisha.

"And me?" asked Max.

"Bashir."

Now there was nothing left to do but go, and Mrs. Pollifax discovered that she did not *want* to go, that for a few hours she had felt safe here in Omar's souk, and that what lay ahead of them couldn't possibly be safe. Worse, somewhere in the journey ahead it was possible—or so Bishop had said—they would meet a face that did not match its photo and that would bring danger indeed. In this strange country of strange customs, with its language strange to her as well, with the police apparently aware of her existence—and the first Janko lying dead in a hut behind them—she could not feel sanguine, she was acquiring a burden of unfocused fear and anxiety.

They walked out into the cool fresh night air. The only lights to be seen came from the hotel on the hill; the village itself was dark and silent. There was no moon but the stars in the great arc of sky were brilliant, and their presence was a comfort to her. The truck loomed large, a vague shape in the night but surely large enough to hold a dozen sheep between its bed-walls. Before climbing into the cab she turned to Omar. "*Shukren,* Omar . . . *Bismallah?*"

"*Bismallah,*" he said gravely. "May Allah go with you."

"It will be hard for you now?"

He shrugged. "Sometimes the saddle is on the man, sometimes the man is on the saddle."

"And what do we say to identify ourselves to the barber in Ourzazate?"

He pointed to Max. "He has it written: you say *Hādha el-husān arej,* the horse has gone lame. Go fast now like the desert wind!"

She climbed up into the cab and Max, already at the wheel, started the engine. "Goodbye, Nadija," she whispered from the window and the truck began to move. "You've forgotten the headlights," she told Max. "Or don't they work?"

"They work," said Max grimly, "but Omar advised against them until we're well away from his house."

She nodded; how foolish of her to have overlooked this, she thought, and as they emerged onto the paved road leading down to the town she fervently hoped the brakes worked well, too. They coasted noiselessly down the hill, the brakes efficiently curtailing their speed, and after passing shadowy alleys and darkened souks they left Tinehir behind.

II. *They* were both shivering in the pre-dawn chill as they began their drive toward Ourzazate. "Just think," Max said sadly, "on the other side of the mountains—" He removed one hand from the wheel to gesture westward. "At sea level it's warm and green and fertile, and the Atlantic Ocean rims the entire coast, with waves breaking against beaches . . ."

"Stop," she said, placing her hands over her ears.

"And in Marrakech there are palm trees, and one of the most elegant hotels in the world, and—"

"Playground of the rich," she scoffed.

"Yes, with its huge plaza called Djemma-el-Fna, where snake charmers and acrobats perform and—"

"No beggars?" she asked skeptically.

"Oh lots," he said cheerfully. "Pickpockets, too."

She did not want to think of Marrakech. "How far is it to Ourzazate?"

"If Allah and this truck are with us we should be there by noon—Insh'allah."

"By daylight then," she said in relief. "Good!"

They had driven only a few miles from Tinehir when they saw moving toward them the twin lights of a truck, and then as the road curved gently Mrs. Pollifax counted five more pairs of headlights in convoy. She said quickly, "Max—"

"I see them." His voice was sober. "It's still dark but keep your face veiled."

"They could be going to market," she pointed out.

"Five in a row?"

The trucks neared them, drew abreast, each one illuminated by the lights of its neighbor and there was no mistaking the size or color of them, they bore the square-cut drab chassis and squared canvas tops of the military. It was unnerving; she reminded herself that Emily Pollifax and Max Janko had been left behind in Tinehir, they were now two Berbers in a scarred and patched-up Volvo, their names Aisha and Bashir, but she did not count it an auspicious beginning to this new day.

"What do you think," said Max edgily. "Military maneuvers or roadblock?"

"I think in the long run," she told him, "it's kinder to assume the worst, don't you?"

He said in a depressed voice, "I guess so."

She remembered that he'd not slept at all during the night but had helped Omar to load his truck; it seemed a good moment to divert him. "I'm wondering where Omar and Nadija are now," she told him. "With his rugs and his wondrous brass charcoal brazier, and I'm wondering what will happen to Nadija. What future do young girls have here?"

"Not much of one," said Max. "Well, I can tell you what her future would be if she'd remained in Tinehir." He shrugged. "She'd be marrying in two or three years, and the marriage would be an arranged one, and probably not a very good one if Omar's a *barānīs*—an outsider. Unfortunately a girl nearly always lives with her husband's family, which—given the position of women here—creates a lot of jealousy and competition and contributes to half the marriages in this country ending in divorce."

"Half!" she said in astonishment.

He nodded. "That's what my statistics tell me. Actually her future should be a hell of a lot brighter in the desert with the Polisarios, where a rather extraordinary thing has been happening, considering it's an Islamic society there, too. With the men off fighting the women have been left to run the affairs at home —they have to! No veils, no cloister, they've set up schools in their city of tents and some of the women fight along with the men as well."

"They're being treated as human beings?" she said in surprise. "How incredible. I've not wanted to mention it but I've been growing hungry for the sight of a woman. Just one. With the exception of the tourists in Erfoud I've seen no adult women unless those bundles in black that we passed were women."

"Believe," he said. "Enormous waste, of course, it's doubtful that many in this part of the country have gone to school or learned to read and write. I doubt if Nadija's ever gone to school, for that matter—there's no compulsory education in Morocco, and you can see how she helps her father. Sewing and cooking and childbearing is about the size of their horizon. And gossiping."

"But there will be school for Nadija in the desert?"

"If she wants it, yes," he said. "I like all the things I hear about them. One of your American senators visited their tent city at Tindouf in Algeria before such connections were severed. He was certainly impressed. If I remember correctly he was quoted as saying he'd never met with such discipline, cohesion and sense of nationhood before . . . They simply want their land back."

"And nobody listens."

He shook his head and was silent, his head silhouetted now against a softly brightening sky. It was dawn, and soon the sun rose, spreading a golden light over the land and they drove under a sky of intense blue, interrupted only by long thin wisps of cloud that laced the distant mesas in the east. In the foreground the sun illuminated a terrain that seemed to Mrs. Pollifax to bubble and swirl toward them, so precisely arranged in scallop after scallop of low green hills that altogether it gave the illusion of being in motion. Then the small hills vanished, the earth flattened and turned again to grainy sand. They passed through the town of Boumaine-Dades glowing in the sun, its tawny buildings like children's play-cubes marching up a matching tawny hill. The road curved and began climbing toward other grassless sand-colored hills.

As they approached El Kelaa Max said abruptly, "I don't like to be negative but how are we fixed for money after buying this truck?"

She hesitated, sorry that he'd brought up the subject. "Not well. I'm loaded with traveler's checks, of course—"

"—which to cash would bring the police down on our heads."

"Yes. I've American money in cash but would it be safe to use that?"

He frowned. "Highly doubtful. How would two poor citizens such as we are—Aisha and Bashir—have received U.S. currency? What have you left in Moroccan money?"

She brought her purse from under her djellabah and counted. "Four hundred fifty dirhams."

He made a face. "That's about fifty-two dollars in American money and I've not much more . . . looks like a sardine-and-oranges diet for us ad nauseam." He gave her a quick sidelong glance. "You could nap, you know. You're doing pretty damn well, considering you were nearly killed yesterday and had only a few hours' sleep last night on Omar's floor. I can wake you when we get to Ourzazate."

"I should," she agreed, "except that not knowing what lies ahead of us in Ourzazate makes it surprisingly difficult to relax, not to mention sleep."

"I take it you're thinking not just of the police but of the rotten apple in the barrel?"

She nodded.

"Look," he said, "has it occurred to you, do you think it possible that Flavien was the rotten apple? He could have been the imposter, in which case all the remaining informants will check out okay."

"Lovely thought," she told him wistfully but after considering it she shook her head. "It was definitely implied by Carstairs' assistant that misleading *information* had begun arriving through the network, which is what prompted them sending us here, and Flavien had no access to the Polisario network. He didn't even know who the informants were until I shared their names with him."

"Still," he began.

"Don't, Max."

"No wishful thinking allowed?" he asked with a smile.

"Not in this business," she told him with an answering smile.

"Then I'll be quiet," he said meekly.

Perversely she found his silence disagreeable now that he'd brought up the scarcity of money, for it encouraged the flow of even more worrisome problems, such as how on earth they would ever get *OUT* of Morocco with the police looking for them, and with the pair of them driving deeper each day into the countryside and further away from cities and airports. In fact, she thought, as one negative begat another, there was

Muhammed Tuhami the barber to worry about, the elderliness of the Volvo truck, the diminishing money supply as well as their hoped-for exit, and adding up all the uncertainties she said at last, very firmly, "Oh to hell with it."

"I beg your pardon!" gasped Max.

She laughed. "Did I startle you? I didn't realize I'd said that out loud, I simply decided to stop worrying." And having announced this they promptly acquired a fresh worry as the Volvo began to protest the steepness of the hill they were climbing. Max pressed the accelerator to the floor, a few minutes later shifted into second gear and then as the truck continued slowing he switched into low gear. When they reached the crest they each of them gave a sigh of relief but the experience had not been encouraging.

They reached Ourzazate in early afternoon, their hunger not entirely appeased by oranges and sardines but at least reduced to a reasonable level. Entering the town Mrs. Pollifax found herself again disoriented as they drove down a broad and tree-lined avenue past several luxury hotels, followed by restaurants and a cafe, a post office, a bookstore, an imposing bank. The contrast was too startling to assimilate all at once.

"Very French Colonial," murmured Max. "Definitely the French have been here."

"It's certainly—well, European," she agreed.

"And too damn European for that barber we look for. Read aloud for me—very slowly—the address you wrote down for me." He handed over the slip of memo paper on which she'd printed names and towns.

"Muhammed Tuhami, barber . . . corner Street of The Makers of Felt Hats and Street of The Barbers, on way to Great Mosque."

He nodded. "Definitely there has to be an older section, there couldn't possible be a Street of The Makers of Felt Hats here, the French wouldn't have allowed it. We'd better drive around . . . We can't afford the gas but we can't afford to stop and ask questions either."

They drove up and down streets lined with walled villas until Max gave a shout of triumph. Pointing he said, "Look ahead—native life triumphs over the Colonial!"

She nodded, smiling as she saw familiar adobe buildings and clusters of men in djellabahs. They passed two men riding donkeys, both seated side-saddle to accommodate the huge burlap sacks laced to one side, and as they drove nearer, "Not a medina," she announced, pleased at her growing knowledge. "No covered alleys, it's an open marketplace."

"Yes, let's park and walk. He's got to be here, this is where the real business takes place."

"Do we look for him as Aisha and Bashir, or as tourists?" she asked. "Frankly I think we should go back to being tourists, I don't see any women."

He made a face. "Confusing, isn't it? But you're right, it would cause too much attention, a native woman walking with a man, any native women would be accompanied by another woman. And we're both wearing the wrong shoes, a dead giveaway."

"As tourists we'll bring attention, too, of course."

"But a different sort." He nodded. "I'll park around the corner on a side street and we can quietly become Westerners again."

A few minutes later, with the truck parked and locked, a pair of tourists, aunt and nephew, strolled toward the marketplace. At once a swarm of boys came running, hands outstretched, but Max waved them away.

"You gave before," she reminded him.

"A good Moslem does, the Koran says strong things about giving to the poor," he retorted, "but at this moment I'm not a good Moslem. Give them a few coins and we'd be trailed all the way to Muhammed. If we can find him."

"We have to," she said quietly.

They entered the dusty square that was framed and walled by flat-roofed open stalls, interrupted here and there by thread-like alleys leading out of the market. It was certainly different from the main street of the town and Mrs. Pollifax much preferred its color and vitality. In a far corner a group of men surrounded a herd of goats, arguing and gesticulating as they bargained. The market stalls held crates of sardines bedded in ice, piles of oranges, as well as tomatoes, fresh herbs, pots and pans, shoes and tall white plastic jugs of cooking oil for sale. For the most part the djellabahs matched the brown of the earth but a few boys could be seen wearing Western-style zip-up jackets of bright red or blue.

"Look, I've got to find the equivalent of a men's room," said Max, and looking around the square he added, "Dreary thought. Wait for me here, will you?"

"Of course." She watched him go bounding away, pause to ask directions of a boy and then vanish down an alley. Finding a low wall behind her she sat down to enjoy the sun and the scene around her. At once three young boys ran up to her, two of them making what looked to be scribbling motions in their hands. The third child only watched shyly.

"A pen?" she asked. They looked blank, and delving into her purse she brought out an inexpensive plastic pen.

Their response was startled, baffled, and as they again scribbled into their palms the shopkeeper in the souk behind her darted out and shooed them angrily away, and without so much as a glance at Mrs. Pollifax returned to his shop.

She realized that what they'd wanted was money, of course, it was simply that here in the south the hand-motions had changed. She dropped the pen back into her purse, appalled by her naivete.

The third child had not gone far; he stood watching her with curiosity, and there was something about him that caught at her heart; his eyes were huge in his small face, he was thin as a sparrow, barefooted, his khaki shorts too long and his T-shirt too large. *He looks lonely,* she thought, *and he didn't beg, he only watched, he's different.*

She saw Max emerging from an alley. She glanced quickly at the shopkeeper behind her, engaged now in conversation with a friend. Reaching into her change purse she drew out a two-dirham coin and with a smile at the watching boy she put a finger to her lips and conspicuously placed the coin on the wall beside her. As she rose to meet Max the boy darted up behind her and snatched the coin. When she turned to look again he had not fled; he stood his ground and gave her a dazzling smile, as if the two of them had outwitted the shopkeeper and shared a conspiracy. Lifting two fingers to his lips he blew her a kiss.

Charmed, she blew a kiss back to him.

"Now who the heck are you tossing kisses to?" asked Max, looking amused.

She only smiled and shook her head. "Shall we go? I count six alleys to explore."

"Mercifully with street signs," he said, and grasping her arm he led her past a stall of oranges to the nearest alley with a sign affixed to the wall. Its swirls and curlicues of Arabic struck her as almost musical in their grace.

"*Assammarin,*" read Max. "That translates as Street of The Horseshoers, let's move on."

Next came The Street of Sellers of Silk Thread, and after peering down it they strolled on to the next cobbled exit.

"*Al-hajjamin,*" he read. "Hooray—we've found The Street of The Barbers!"

She said nervously, "Does that mean dozens of barbers to inspect?"

He grinned. "Probably fifty years ago it did but I doubt it now. Care to describe our man before we set out?"

She stopped and closed her eyes to concentrate. "Younger than Omar, perhaps only thirty or thirty-two. A short dark beard, pale oval face, short and thin in size. In the photo he wore a shabby striped djellabah. Looked intense—very intense —also poor."

Max nodded. "He would be, yes. I'm mainly a translater and decoder, but the Maghreb's my specialty and—"

"Maghreb?"

"Morocco, Algeria and Tunisia . . . But aside from translating I do know that in this country a barber's ranked very low on the social scale—considered almost beyond the pale, so to speak—and yet because he provides important news and gossip he has a popularity in spite of his profession. In barber shops people talk and people listen."

"Perfect for an informant! So there's a caste system here?"

"Not really," he said. "This is a country of tribes, and the old ways linger, it's a matter of which tribe you come from and whether you're related to any saints or descended from Mohammed's brother-in-law Ali. Even the poorest of poor can be treated with great respect if they've important connections."

They passed a shop filled with displays of leather purses, a man cutting leather at a counter; a shop with two men pedaling away at sewing machines, and a narrow souk displaying slippers in rainbow colors with curled and pointed toes. "Barouches," commented Max. As they strolled nearer to the end of the street there was a promise of sunshine and space ahead; at the corner they found waiting for them a sign bearing an outline of scissors, with the same curls of Arabic beneath it.

"Keep your fingers crossed," growled Max.

This shop had a dusty glass window and door, and they stopped to peer inside. The barber's room was very small but clean and bright, which pleased her. A single chair, gloriously old and ornate, stood rooted in the center of the room, its seat covered with red plush; it rested on a base of elaborate iron scrollwork so deliciously intricate that it reminded Mrs. Pollifax of Victorian gingerbread. It was a handsome old barber-chair and she thought it a sight to bring a gleam of covetousness to the eyes of an antique dealer. There was a mirror on the wall that had been corroded by time and mildew and shared space with a photograph of Mohammed V and of the present King. There was a rough bench for any waiting customers.

A client already occupied the glorious chair but the barber himself had his back to the window. "Suspense mounts," she murmured, but at that moment the man turned and she breathed a deep sigh of relief. "Reprieved again," she whispered. "That's Muhammed Tuhami."

"Sure?"

She nodded.

"Let's go in, I'll pretend I need a trim."

The entry of tourists—and one of them a woman—startled the two occupants of the shop. Nodding politely Max guided her to the bench and they sat down. To the barber he said, "I need a trim. Do you speak English?"

Observing Muhammed, Mrs. Pollifax thought he looked both older and wearier since his photograph had been taken for the gallery of informants, but his intensity had not diminished even when he said cautiously, "A little. *Parlez-vous français?*"

Max at once began speaking in fluent French and Mrs. Pollifax sighed, her curiosity boundless but thwarted. Muhammed laughed once, a little weakly; the occupant of the chair, swathed in towels, smiled, and in an aside Max told her, "I'm telling them that as tourists we brought swimming suits but have met with much cold."

"Ah yes, the weather as usual," she murmured.

Towels were unfurled and Muhammed's customer rose, obviously a man of prosperity for he wore a white djellabah over well-pressed Western slacks and shirt. Coins were bestowed on Muhammed, he bowed to Max, gave Mrs. Pollifax a curious glance and went out, closing the door behind him.

There was silence. Muhammed held out towels to Max and waited. Max said slowly, carefully, "The horse has gone lame . . . *Hādha el-husān arej.*"

To Mrs. Pollifax's surprise Muhammed's facial expression showed not the slightest astonishment; with the greatest competence he went to the door and locked it, pulled down its steel shutters and returned. In the dimness they examined one another, Muhammed silent and waiting.

Max said, "We come from Omar's souk in Tinehir. We come to tell you the chain—the network—has been broken."

"Omar," repeated Muhammed, nodding. "But—" He looked puzzled. "Omar is brawkin?"

With apologies to Mrs. Pollifax Max returned to French but she found that by watching Muhammed's face she could guess something of what was being said to him. There was a widening of eyes, a look of horror—perhaps that was Hamid ou Azu's murder—followed by a narrowing of eyes—she thought now he was learning of the first Janko's identity—and then a startled glance at Mrs. Pollifax, which prompted her to assume that Max's synopsis had reached the saint's tomb and Flavien's death. When the words Tinehir and Omar were spoken, his face softened and he spoke.

Max, translating, said, "He is happy to hear that Omar has left for the desert. Now of course I have to tell him that he's in danger, too. I don't think this has hit him yet."

This was explained to Muhammed, which took a few minutes, and for the first time Mrs. Pollifax saw his eyes register alarm and then fear. "No, no," he protested, backing away from them. "I cannot go—cannot."

"It could be dangerous to stay."

"Yes, yes I comprehend but—" He broke into French again and Max sighed. Translating he said, "He tells me his wife is sick. He says that Allah has blessed him with a pearl of a wife and there is love between them. He says she cannot be moved and he can't leave her."

"Oh dear," murmured Mrs. Pollifax, and felt a stab of compassion for him. He impressed her as an ordinary man with ordinary worries and concerns. He was probably trembling on the edge of poverty, barely making ends meet, and caring for a sick wife and yet something—and she wondered what—had turned him into an uncommon man and set him apart from his neighbors. There looked nothing of the rebel about him, yet very firmly he had adopted a dangerous secret life, and entirely without recompense. She wondered what had altered his way of thinking: was it an injustice done to him here in this country, or had he friends among the Polisarios, or did he belong to a tribe that had once slept under the stars in the desert? She said gently, "It could be all right, you know, Max. If Muhammed is known only to the man ahead of us, in Zagora, and the man in Zagora turns out to match his photo—"

"Talk about wishful thinking!" Max exclaimed. "We're down to the last two possibilities, you're talking Russian roulette now."

She turned to Muhammed. "Ask him if he's heard lately from the south, from the man in Zagora?"

He moved to the calendar on the wall with the Islamic year 1410 in huge letters at the top. His finger found a month and traced the numbers until he met with a small *x* in the corner and spoke.

"He says three weeks ago," Max told her, translating. "A longer silence than usual, he admits."

"Sounds rather ominous," she said uneasily. "He *must* do something to protect himself. Tell him he has to see the danger and think of his wife if he should be taken away!"

Muhammed lifted a hand and gestured. "Come," he said. "I show." He lifted a curtain in the rear, exposing a doorway, and led them down a short passageway into a small dim room in which half a dozen women in black huddled around the sick woman. At their appearance the shapeless black shadows rose and fled the room, leaving only Muhammed's wife lying on a mat.

Muhammed spoke to her softly and beckoned Mrs. Pollifax to come forward. Joining him she looked down at his wife. She was strikingly beautiful, like a Madonna with eyes made huge by kohl; she smiled and with a welcoming gesture reached out a hand.

Mrs. Pollifax grasped and held it. "Shukren—and hello," she stammered. "Max, what's wrong?"

"She lost a child four days ago, Muhammed tells me. It was upside down in her womb and born dead. It's a wonder she survived."

"Was there a doctor?"

"Midwife. Now his wife is very weak, she lacks strength and—"

"—and spirit," finished Mrs. Pollifax. She looked thoughtfully at Muhammed's wife and then reached into her voluminous purse to bring out her large jar of multi-vitamin tablets, followed by a 200-dirham note, the equivalent of twenty-five dollars in American currency. Handing Muhammed the jar she said, "Please, two of these pills—" She lifted two fingers. "Two each day, and with this money a doctor, and perhaps more food."

He backed away but Mrs. Pollifax was stern. "For you *no*, Muhammed. This is for your wife, the pearl that Allah sent you, so that you can have choice—to go, or to hide, or to stay."

"But so much," he gasped, as he saw the size of the bill, and lifting his eyes to Mrs. Pollifax he said softly, "You speak of Allah, you have to have been sent by Allah." He placed a hand over his heart. "Shukren, madame."

"Now we must go," Mrs. Pollifax reminded Max. "It's already afternoon and if we don't hurry—it's a hundred more miles to Zagora, isn't it?—we'll never reach it today."

He nodded and told this to Muhammed. "Maybe for a few days your shop should stay closed?"

Muhammed nodded absently; he was looking at his wife. "If Allah wills it," he murmured, "if strength returns . . . We are *barānīs* here—outsiders—but perhaps in a few days, with money, there may be a way to go." He turned to them and said with dignity, "You give us hope. May Allah's blessings go with you, sir and madame."

They had reached the door to the street when he called out to them, "Wait! Stop!"

They turned.

"There is *fabor*—" He spoke hurriedly and with passion in French and she thought that Max looked alarmed.

"What is it?" she asked.

"After innumerable apologies," said Max, "he explains that while he must stay with his wife there is a boy, their only son. He offers the money back—anything—if we will take the boy with us to Zagora, to the house of his wife's sister, because if there is danger it is wise that he go."

She said quickly, "But of course we can do that, can't we, Max? Tell him to keep his money and yes—*oui*—the boy can go with us."

Max made a gesture of comic helplessness. "The lady—" he told Muhammed "—Tante *Emily, my 'amma,* says *oui.*"

"Ahhhh," murmured Muhammed, and the murmur contained all the pent-up tension of his suspense as he had waited, it spoke more than words of his accumulating anxieties. "Thank you, thank you, he has just come back. He is nine years old, named Ahmad, I call him."

"No, tell us first where to deliver him. The directions," Max said, bringing out notebook and pencil, and Muhammed exploded into Arabic and French and then disappeared to fetch the boy.

"Here he is," he said almost immediately.

The boy emerged from the shadows of the passageway, his eyes fixed shyly on Mrs. Pollifax. Seeing him she laughed. "But already we've met! This is your son Ahmad?"

It needed several moments of explanation to establish the fact that Mrs. Pollifax was the tourist-lady who had given Ahmad two dirhams with which he had bought sweets and oranges for his mother.

Muhammed's eyes glowed at this and he nodded. "He likes you early—*bon!*" With much pride he added, "He knows the English kinder than me, you will see. Ahmad, by tonight you will be in Zagora with your 'amma."

"Only if we start now," pointed out Max. "Tell him he must walk behind us until we reach our truck where we will change into djellabahs and not be tourists any more."

Muhammed embraced his son and murmured into his ear; Mrs. Pollifax recognized only the words *Allah* and *Bismallah,* and then Muhammed opened the door to them. *"Nehna abid Allah,"* he said to Max.

Max gravely nodded. "Yes, we are all servants of Allah. Goodbye, Muhammed, and be careful."

◎

12 . *Leaving* the barber shop still as tourists, with Ahmad keeping his distance behind them, they took the time to stop at a souk and buy plastic sandals, and then to invest in what food they could travel with, which turned out to be more oranges, tins of sardines, black olives, two bottles of mineral water and five of cola, all of which further depleted their funds. They were followed out of the marketplace by a troop of beggar boys so rapacious that at last it became necessary to appeal to Ahmad to send them away, since the sight of tourists climbing into such an ancient truck would become a rare topic of conversation and only too well remembered if they were interviewed later.

Ahmad turned on the boys and spat words at them.

"What is he saying?" she asked.

Max grinned. "We have corrupted the boy, he is shouting curses at them."

"Such as?"

"Perhaps the most picturesque curses were 'May God give you fever' and 'May God give you fever without perspiration."

Suppressing a grin Mrs. Pollifax said with dignity, "Thank you, Ahmad, thank you."

Once rid of the begging boys they pointed out their truck to Ahmad, and its appearance obviously excited him; he climbed inside to reverently touch the steering wheel and then to stroke the gear shift, smiling a smile of deep contentment. When he glanced at Max and Mrs. Pollifax and saw them changing clothes he watched Mrs. Pollifax's clumsy entanglement with her veil. "No, no," he said, in high humor at seeing them change from *nasrani* to native, and with a grin he secured it carefully for her. He brought a holiday feeling to this departure that was unfortunately brief because the guidebook hinted at new mountains ahead before they reached the plains, and already it was doubtful that they could reach Zagora before dark. There had been no hint of mountains on their map and it was the guidebook that proved accurate. Heading south toward the desert, and the border again, the first lap of their journey was precipitous, taking them high above the river Draa. From a dizzying height Mrs. Pollifax looked down with tightened nerves on the narrow green valley through which the river ran, as serpentine as the road over which they drove, which had been carved out of a cliff thousands of feet above. The valley was fertile, the goats and sheep clinging to the steep green slopes and grazing, but it was impossible to appreciate such a pastoral scene when she could only think how easily they might hurtle down to join them.

But if the Volvo panted and groaned it didn't falter. It had acquired a personality of its own, she decided, and like the people of the mountains it had adjusted to malnutrition and impoverishment and had grown stubborn and stoic. Ahmad sat between her and Max, his hand holding hers tightly. Occasionally he looked up to smile at her; if his English vocabulary was limited his eyes spoke for him: she had given a two-dirham coin, worth so little, and in return she was being given all the gratitude in his ardent young heart. For him there were no worries about failing brakes or steering mechanisms, his trust was total.

Max, however, had begun to look haggard. They might have nursed the hope of reaching Zagora before nightfall but there was no pushing the truck and there began to be shadows in the valley below and then across the road as the sun sank lower in the sky.

"We're not going to make it to Zagora," she said at last, flatly.

"We'll be damn lucky to finish with these hairpin curves while it's still light," he growled.

It was with great relief that they coasted down the last hill and looked ahead to a darkening road that stretched for miles across a flat landscape.

"Thank God," said Max.

She nodded. "We've got to stop, we don't know what's ahead in Zagora and we need sleep, food and daylight."

He gave her a quick glance. "Quite."

They began to look for a place to camp that was concealed from the road. They passed a cluster of houses where the black silhouette of a woman could be seen carrying a load of firewood on her back, and then a mile further along they came upon a grove of olive trees. Max drove the truck in among the trees and when they were well hidden he turned off the engine. The silence was profound: they could hear neither cars nor people nor even bird calls; it was the hush before sunset.

"I think," said Max grimly, "that following today's driving my nerves ought to be well honed for the Grand Prix. The tires on this truck are threadbare, the wheel alignment crazy, the brakes suspenseful and we've maneuvered roads today that had more curves than a belly dancer."

Ahmad gave him a happy glance. "When I grow big I will be driver of truck, too."

Mrs. Pollifax smiled at him. "He certainly watched you like a hawk, Max, every move that you made. Come, let's eat and we'll feel better. There's the tarpaulin in the back and the ragged blanket Omar left for us, we'll sleep under the stars."

They climbed down from the cab and into the rear of the truck, carrying their food with them. Seated cross-legged in the deepening twilight they opened tins of sardines and distributed colas. If Mrs. Pollifax found herself growing rather tired of sardines and oranges she only had to observe how eagerly Ahmad ate his ration to feel humbled.

"By the way," said Max, giving her a thoughtful glance, "I don't like to bring up disagreeable subjects while we're eating—it's hell on the digestion, of course—but I'd like to point out that we're coming nearer to the end of the list, and, if one of these remaining two chaps turns out to be the villain of the piece, has it occurred to you that we can scarcely follow instructions and visit a post office to send a cable when the police must be looking for us now, and every post office, bank and hotel alerted?"

She said quietly, "Of course it's occurred to me, a number of problems have occurred to me."

"*Problems?*" he mocked. "*Problems?*"

"You're tired," she pointed out.

"Did *you* know what you'd be getting into?" he asked indignantly. "Did you have any idea we'd be on the lam, so to speak, and the police after us?"

"Of course not, Bishop told me it was to be a pleasant drive through the real Morocco doing nothing but matching seven people to seven photographs."

"That makes me feel like laughing hysterically."

"Some sleep would be more practical," she pointed out. "Although if you feel like laughing hysterically go ahead, but quietly."

"Oh damn, where's the blanket?" he grumbled, and when

she handed it to him he lay down and his eyes immediately closed.

They slept huddled together under the blanket and the tarpaulin, warmed by body heat, and for many hours too exhausted to feel the encroaching chill of a January night in the open. When the cold woke Mrs. Pollifax it was still dark and she realized that Max was no longer lying next to Ahmad.

"Max?" she faltered.

"Still here," came his voice cheerfully from the end of the truck. "Doing push-ups to get warm." He walked back and she saw him silhouetted against the dark sky before he sat down and pulled his share of blanket over his lap. "Oh for a cup of coffee! What time is it?"

"Half-past three."

"You slept, I hope?"

"Gloriously, and now it's suddenly Thursday. We wait for daylight to leave?"

"Think we'd better, don't you? It should be dawn in another hour. We can tell stories."

She smiled. "Do you know a good one?"

He thought a moment. "I don't know whether it's a good one but it's a story that's haunted me ever since I began learning about the Maghreb, its adventurers and history and cultures. It's a story about real people, a vignette that I cherish."

"Tell me," she urged.

"I'm thinking how to tell it," he said, "because it's a matter of defining character before one can appreciate the overwhelming irony and surprise of it. Have you heard the name Lyautey? General Lyautey?"

She frowned. "I think—yes, when I looked over the short history of Morocco in the guidebook it was very prominent."

Max nodded. "He was the first resident-general of Morocco

after the French triumphed at last and made it a protectorate in 1912. But he began his career years earlier in Algeria, which was already colonized by the French. Lyautey was the sort of man whose ambitions and talents were larger than any connections he had in France, and he quite sensibly chose the Colonial service. He was assigned an outpost in Ain-Sefra, in the Algerian desert, where his job was to prevent the fierce Moroccan tribes from crossing the border to raid his supply lines.

"Okay," he said, settling down to his story. "Picture if you will an aristocratic type, intellectual, an egoist, with no interest in women or the time and patience for friends. Brilliant, of course. Fastidious, forceful, hard on his men, exacting, demanding . . ."

She smiled. "I get the picture."

"Good. And now I ask if you've ever heard the name of Isabelle Eberhardt?"

Again she frowned. "An explorer, wasn't she? Or one of those Victorian women travelers?"

"A traveler certainly, but she was also—" He hesitated. "Also a rebel, an astonishing rebel—to the point of self-destruction, one might say—and eventually an outcast of society. After a visit to North Africa as a young woman it captured her heart and soul and she returned, converted to Islam, married a native of Algeria—you can imagine the furor that caused in the early century—and then left him and began her wanderings. She dressed like a man and called herself Si Mahmoud, becoming a nomad herself and wandering about with the tribes, often scorned by both Europeans and Algerians."

Max stopped and then, "It is said that one night when he was returning to his tent General Lyautey stumbled over a man curled up asleep in a blanket, a man who called himself Si Mahmoud."

"Isabelle Eberhardt!"

"Yes. And learning who she was—she was somewhat infamous by that time—he invited her into his tent and they talked until dawn. It is said that every night following that she returned to his tent and they talked—about what who can tell, this outcast of a woman who had flouted every rule of Victorian society, and this fastidious, seemingly cold and correct man.

"And it has been said," he added, "that in his entire life Lyautey claimed to have found only one true friendship, and—brief as it was—it was with this woman."

But she had caught the word *brief*. "Why brief?"

"She was killed in a mudslide some months later in that remote outpost of Ain-Sefra—she was twenty-eight years old."

Mrs. Pollifax was silent, and Max waited for her response. "She must have been searching very hard for something," she said softly. "She sounds a passionate and a troubled woman, but it's as if fate had smiled a little on her, don't you think? As if she was drawn to that village in the desert to die—but first to meet and know this man and to affect his life, and to perhaps—who knows?—be understood for the first time in her own life. What a strange story, Max!"

"I collect strange stories," he said. "I just hope that I'm not going to be a character in one of them before this week ends."

The darkness had thinned enough for her to see the flash of his smile but it was not a happy smile. From the road beyond the olive grove she heard the sound of a truck passing; in another hour it would be daylight and they would again try to reach Zagora and look for informant number six, whose name was Sidi Tahar Bouseghine, and who sold carpets. She shivered, and Max said, "Cold?"

In a small depressed voice she said, "I think I'd better try a few push-ups, too."

13 • *Mornajay* flew into Marrakech on the after-noon plane, still somewhat annoyed by the interruption of his holiday in Spain but growing increasingly curious as to what he might discover or even manage to accomplish in Morocco. He felt a challenge here that took him back to youthful days when he was working his way up through the ranks of a burgeoning CIA and frequently arrived in unfriendly cities with nothing but the name of a contact who might or might not be helpful or even accessible. He carried with him the list of the seven towns that Carstairs had spelled out for him over the phone, as well as the names of the seven informants, and by drawing discreetly on his considerable resources he had the name of a young chap in Marrakech whom he thought he could question without giving away his reasons for being here. It was one reason why he had chosen Marrakech as his base of operations, the other being its proximity to the land beyond the High Atlas.

He was wearing an immaculately tailored white suit that set off his large head with its mane of thick leonine gray hair, about which he was admittedly vain, and his six days in Spain had given his face a tan that lent a semblance of warmth to his cold gray eyes. It was a full year since an abrupt message from Thailand had removed him from his desk to experience a per-sonal tragedy that had somewhat softened him but he was still a man of ice, only a little less disliked, and only a shade less egotistical. In every official capacity he was Carstairs' superior at the CIA but it was a mark of the change in him that where the Atlas group was concerned he shared authority with four other men.

From the airport he took a cab to the Hotel Mamounia where he'd reserved a room, and this at once lifted his spirits. He had a distinct appetite for luxury and the hotel, recently renovated, was like a journey into the Arabian Nights, with a soupçon of Art Deco to flavor it. Once in his room he made a call to one Kenneth Bartlett, announcing his presence and his visit inside the hour, and following this he ordered a car to rent for his supposed week of sight-seeing. Before taking possession of it he changed into more casual clothes, drew out a small bag into which he packed binoculars, two sweaters, boots, a windbreaker and wool cap, shaving gear and what in every way resembled a camera but was actually a gun, and a second camera to more conspicuously wear over his shoulder. Carrying his bag he strolled through the vast lobby with its mirrors, couches and statuary, and after signing papers for the Renault he checked his map and set out to find his contact Kenneth Bartlett.

Since the CIA's presence in Morocco was technically a secret—in general, Congress would not be pleased—he found his man in a dusty office just off the Avenue Mohammed V, on the second floor over an outdoor cafe. The office door bore the usual ubiquitous sign IMPORTS. Opening it he was confronted by a clutter of file cabinets and computers, wall maps and books and two desks, only one of them occupied. A closed door led to a second room that he guessed was the Communications Room. Young Bartlett rose from the nearer desk and held out his hand. "Mr. Mornajay, sir, it's a real honor," he said, his freckled face beaming.

Mornajay was pleased that his instincts had proven sound: Bartlett looked not long out of university, untested as yet, and the sort of young man more addicted to statistics and computers than to derring-do. He shook the proffered hand, dropped into the chair next to the desk and repeated with elaborate casualness the fact that he was on vacation, stopping merely to pay his respects and to perhaps receive a few recommendations on where to dine and what to see.

"Well, of course the Djemma-el-Fna," Bartlett said eagerly, "although if you stop to watch anything they want money. It's also where Jenkins"—he gestured toward the empty desk beside him—"had his pocket picked but I can recommend driving past it at night when every stall's lighted by lanterns and it's like seeing a whole field of fireflies in the darkness."

Not *entirely* statistics, amended Mornajay.

"And of course the Koutoubia—the tower's famous—except you can't go inside."

Mornajay pretended a few scribbles in a notebook and said smoothly, "I see that you've been making the most of your stay here. Did they give you interesting work? Anything exciting going on at the moment?"

Bartlett looked troubled. "Well yes, there's been a sudden flare-up—it's why Jenkins isn't here. It's a little hard to puzzle out, but the police enlisted our assistance, although I'm not absolutely certain it's the police," he emphasized. "That is, if you know what I mean, sir."

Mornajay assured him that he did.

"It seems a man was found dead up near Erfoud in a mosque or behind it. He'd been shot and his car was abandoned there. But he'd been traveling with a woman, an American woman—"

Nothing changed in Mornajay's face to betray his sudden very intense interest. "An American, you say?"

"—and they think she's the one who murdered him. Anyway she's disappeared, which certainly isn't easy to do in Morocco, at least not for an American and a woman by herself, not to mention there not being many tourists in that part of the country. In January, anyway. It's very mysterious, but what bugs me, sir—"

"Any mention of an accomplice? Any mention of the dead man's identity?" asked Mornajay, his voice sharper.

Bartlett shook his head. "No sir, but what bugs me is—well, I insisted on staying here to man the office, so it was Jenkins who went off to confer with the authorities, but what I'd like to ask is, was I derelict in my duty? The police sounded desperate for help but I couldn't understand why *we*—well, I found I just didn't have the stomach for it, helping to hunt down a woman who's *American*."

"One must of course obey orders," said Mornajay piously, "but in this case I think you were wise to trust your stomach. It's their business. Only when they find the woman does it become our business."

"Thank you, sir," Bartlett said gratefully. "But still it's scarey, you know. They've got a nationwide hunt going on for this Mrs. Pollifax."

Mornajay's eyes narrowed. "Pollifax?" Carstairs had spoken of a woman agent but he'd not attached a name to her. "Did I hear you say *Pollifax?*"

Bartlett nodded. "Odd name, isn't it."

Considerably jarred, Mornajay thought, *It couldn't be, no it's impossible, it has to be someone else.* He heard Bartlett saying that if she could escape far enough south she might run into Americans, for instance the engineers from Westinghouse who were installing electronics on the wall to keep the Polisarios out of Western Sahara, but that was a long *long* way from Erfoud.

Mornajay interrupted him. "Have you a description of this woman?"

Bartlett rose and walked over to Jenkins' desk and removed a sheet of paper. "A very thorough description," he said.

Taking care to keep his voice light and disinterested

Mornajay said, "One wonders how the police or Moroccan Intelligence can describe thoroughly the appearance of a woman they've never seen."

Bartlett shot him a suddenly shrewd glance but said nothing except, "Here we are." And he read aloud a very good description of the woman for whom they were searching.

Good God, thought Mornajay. It was incredible, of course, but it sounded exactly like the woman he'd met in Thailand a year ago, wandering around the mountains looking for a lost husband, except there'd been not the slightest indication of her being anything more than a tourist. It was inconceivable, it was impossible, but he felt a fierce desire to know. He said, "Long-distance calls go through Rabat, I believe, but have you a direct priority line to Virginia?"

"Yes," said Bartlett, looking surprised.

Mornajay nodded. "While I'm here," he said politely, "I wonder if you'd mind if I make a call about a previous matter I'd like an update on."

"Of course." Bartlett shepherded him into the next room and closed the door behind him. Within a few minutes and without interference Mornajay was speaking to Carstairs.

He said smoothly, "I've reached Marrakech and must ask an important question of you before proceeding further. Of the two—er—friends I'm here to look up, one was a woman whose name you did not mention, and I will not mention it now, you understand? But I must know—was that woman in Thailand a year ago in January?"

He heard Carstairs' sudden intake of breath. "What on earth —as a matter of fact yes, but how would you— Good God," he said, sounding stunned, "you were in Thailand that month, too, are you suggesting you *met?*"

He did not reply to this. "She was working for you then? She was working for you that entire time?"

"Yes," said Carstairs, "but you're not answering my question."

Mornajay laughed. "Life has its ironies, certainly! I thought her a damn fool tourist, and told her so, and she assumed I was working for the Drug Enforcement Agency. If it's the same one —and I might add that she's very popular at the moment here, if you follow me—then at least I know who I'm looking for and can assess her resourcefulness."

Carstairs said, "The situation's not good?"

"Not good at all. Needle in a haystack and all that."

"What are you going to do?"

"Haven't the foggiest idea," Mornajay told him, and hung up.

Emerging from the inner room Bartlett glanced up from his computer to say, "Get through all right?" When Mornajay nodded he said, "Sir, do you mind my asking a question that bugs me?"

"By all means. Go ahead."

He scowled. "Well, sir, I realize this country's strategic position on the Mediterranean, and I've been told we can't allow the King here to be toppled like the Shah of Iran, which is why we're here and backing him to the hilt, with American instructors training Moroccan pilots in antimissile tactics, and everybody afraid the war will undermine and weaken the King, but it's still rather fuzzy to me why the Moroccans are *fighting* this war."

"Oh?" said Mornajay encouragingly.

"Yes. I ask people—in cafes and places like that. Moroccans I mean. One of them said the Polisarios are mercenaries hired by Algeria—because Algeria wants a port on an ocean—but that doesn't make sense to me when Algeria has ports on the Mediterranean. Another man said it's because Western Sahara used to be part of Morocco . . ." His scowl deepened as he wrestled with this.

"I think I can do better than that for you," Mornajay said with a tight smile. "Its beginning dates back to 1956 when Morocco achieved its independence from France. In a burst of nationalistic fervor the head of the Istiqlal party, a chap named Allal el-Fassi, announced that Morocco could never be truly unified until it collected unto itself all the countries through which Sultans and Moroccan armies had tramped since the fifteenth and sixteenth centuries." He said dryly, "Considering the hundreds of forays into the desert for gold and slaves, and trading posts set up and abandoned, this embraced quite a bit of territory—for instance, in 1599 Moroccans occupied Timbuktu for a few years but el-Fassi sensibly excluded it because of its poverty and remoteness. He published his map of 'Greater Morocco,' and if people found such extravagant claims laughable at first the King didn't, not with his popularity waning by 1958. Needing a cause he endorsed el-Fassi's so-called claims to a Morocco triple its present size.

"I might add," he said without expression, "that this map of 'Greater Morocco' includes not only Western Sahara but a very large slice of Algeria, the entire country of Mauritania and half the country of Mali. This did not sit well with Algeria, as you can imagine, and it made enemies of them at the time, which is why they've given shelter and aid to the Polisarios. After all, if Morocco takes over Western Sahara, what next?"

Bartlett was staring at him in horror. "But that's insane. You mean that's the reason behind this war that keeps the people so poor here?"

Mornajay lightly patted him on the head. "Never *never* underestimate the lust for power, my dear Bartlett, it makes pawns of most of us, and is prevalent in many corners of this globe. Now if you'll excuse me I shall begin my sight-seeing, with infinite thanks for your counsel."

Bartlett nodded. "My pleasure. Where do you think you'll head first?"

"Oh, I think while the weather's good I might tackle the High Atlas, drive over it by way of the Tizi Pass, and see Zagora before sampling the fleshpots of Marrakech."

Frowning, Bartlett said, "Tizi Pass was closed yesterday due to snow—although of course it may be open by now." He brightened. "When you reach Ourzazate you'll find Jenkins at the Hotel Riad Salaam if you care to look him up."

This was interesting. "That's where they've centered the hunt?" When Bartlett nodded he decided this was very interesting indeed. He waved a hand in farewell and left. He thought that his visit with this young man had produced a fair amount of useful information that he would presently digest as he drove over Tizi-n-Tichka Pass to begin his own search for Mrs. Pollifax.

Mrs. Pollifax . . . He shook his head over this, amazed at learning she was one of Carstairs' agents and was doing a job for Atlas now as well. He still found this hard to believe and yet he conceded that if she'd fooled a professional like himself then it was always possible that she might fool the people hunting for her. He thought the odds against this were as high as Tizi Pass but it was his job now to ferret out a way to reduce those odds.

He left wondering, too, which Max Janko had been killed in Erfoud.

14 • *As* the first fingers of light reached them Ahmad opened his eyes, rubbed them, saw Mrs. Pollifax and sat up smiling. *"Good* day," he said. "We go now in truck?"

"And a good day to you too," she replied, amused. "Will you have an orange?"

"Please thank you," he said. "We go soon in truck?" He stretched out his arms to embrace an imaginary steering wheel and made engine noises . . . *Brummmmm, brummmm, brummmm.*

"Very soon," she assured him. "Have an orange first. Do you go to school, Ahmad?"

"Madrasa," explained Max.

He nodded vigorously. "One time, yes."

"What does that mean?" she asked, and Max set out to inquire. After an animated conversation, with Ahmad bursting into laughter at Max's occasional errors in pronunciation, it was established that Ahmad had gone to school for one full year and one half. "But it was Q'oranic school," said Max, "which is not quite the same, since they almost exclusively teach the Koran there. But he says he can print his name and do sums on the abacus, and from his father and from tourists he has learned some French and English, and when he grows up he would like to be a truck driver. Like me," he added with a roguish grin.

"I hope he drives a newer truck," she said tartly. "How far now?"

"Not far, a couple of hours—*Insh' Allah.* Your guidebook says Zagora is a hill town with a fortress—let's hope not too

135

big a hill—and Ahmad reminds me that his aunt lives on the other side of Zagora, which pleases him because he can stay with us longer."

When she climbed into the truck beside Ahmad he again tucked his hand into hers, trustingly and confidingly. She realized how much she would miss him once he'd been delivered to his aunt. She also wondered what lay ahead for him, uprooted now as he was, and how long it would be before his father came for him. Worst of all she wondered if his father would come for him at all. It was possible that his remaining behind in Ourzazate might doom him if already he'd been betrayed.

Stop, she told herself sternly, *there's work to do,* and *who's to know what will happen to any of us?*

They set out for Zagora with some optimism but today the truck asserted itself. After an hour of driving the radiator boiled over and it was necessary to sit and wait a long time for it to cool. Following this the gasoline gauge turned out to be unreliable, as they discovered when they came to a sudden halt and found the tank empty, after which they spent half an hour prying open the rusted lid on the spare tank for which Omar had bargained. They had expected to reach Zagora by late morning: it was the middle of the afternoon when they found their way to the road leading up from the main street to the hotel.

"Rather neatly removed from the life of the village," murmured Mrs. Pollifax, "but it did say on the back of the photograph 'Sidi Tahar Bouseghine, seller of fine carpets near entrance to Hotel X, Zagora.' "

"His name interests me," said Max, "because Sidi means 'sir' or 'lord' in Morocco, which has to mean he's a sharif." He pulled over to the side of the road and parked so that they could appraise the situation, and Mrs. Pollifax saw that neither the directions nor her memory had failed her: the final approach to the hotel was lined with small souks, five on either side of the road. These had been kept at a discreet distance from its front entrance but they were near enough to give any tourist who cared for a walk the feeling of running a gauntlet.

"What's a sharif?" she asked.

"Descendent of Mohammed, or Ali. What does he look like?"

"Quite Biblical," she told him, remembering the picture. "A turban covered his hair but his beard was white. Not a long beard but enough to give him the look of a patriarch. He didn't realize a photo was being taken of him, he stood in the sun with his arms crossed, watching something or someone, and scowling a little. His face was very dark against the white of his beard, and weathered, but definitely he was not a man to forget, once seen. He had—" She searched for the right word. "He had *presence.*"

Like Cyrus, she thought, smiling.

The hotel stood at the top of the road, crowning it, and was surprisingly palatial for such a provincial town so near to the desert. It was surrounded by gardens, and in the parking apron stood two tour buses, a petit-taxi and a Land Rover with a UK license plate. Seeing this Max backed their truck down to a point below the souks, which proved a reminder to her that as natives they would not be welcomed into this pocket of luxury. He said by way of explanation, "Let's wait here a few minutes and see how things look."

A concierge wearing a long green apron walked out of the hotel entrance, looked up at the sky, turned and went back inside. She said, "There certainly aren't many people to be seen."

"No. Siesta time perhaps?"

"This will make us conspicuous . . ."

"Yes, rather."

She said uneasily, "I count ten shops, five on each side of the street, which means a lot of reconnoitering."

"Yes," he said, looking troubled.

I'm nervous, very nervous, she thought, *it really is like Russian roulette now.* They had come so far—somehow—and now they were very near to the end and the odds had increased against them with each hour and at every stop. Time was their enemy now, as well as the police, and possibly one of these last two informants.

Max interrupted her thoughts. "Why don't I do the reconnoitering? I can peer inside each souk and look for a man with a white beard, and when I find him—"

If, she thought tiredly.

"—you can join me and see if he's the Sidi Tahar Bouseghine in your photograph."

"And would you go as Max or as Bashir?"

"Good question." He was silent, and Ahmad turned his head to look at each of them in turn, puzzled by the doubts he sensed.

"We appear to have reached a nadir," said Mrs. Pollifax.

Max sighed. "You're right. A cold night spent in a truck and a diet of snacks slows the brain. I'd better go as Bashir, I guess. It doesn't seem possible they'd be circulating a description of me but there's no point in taking chances. No more tourism for me, I'll stay Bashir."

"Take Ahmad with you," she suggested, and smiled down at his eager face. "He'll be excellent cover."

"Cover?" teased Ahmad, with his shy smile. "Like a blanket?"

"Yes, because you'll help Max look Moroccan."

"Not like *nasrani,*" Ahmad said, nodding wisely. "You are frightened, *madehm?*"

"This kid is too wise," growled Max.

"We're nervous, Ahmad," she told him.

"Oh . . . *kay*. We go?"

Max grinned. "Yes, Ahmad, we go."

They climbed out of the truck and Mrs. Pollifax sat and watched them as they crossed the street to begin their search among the shops on the left. Five times they vanished briefly, not lingering, and five times reappeared. Before approaching the shops on the opposite side Max returned to say with cheerful efficiency, "Two black beards, one moustache and one clean-shaven, no Sidi Tahar."

She gravely thanked him and they left to reconnoiter the remaining five souks. It was when they emerged from the last one, the one nearest to the truck, that Mrs. Pollifax saw Max smiling. He lifted his fingers in a *V* sign as he walked toward her with Ahmad at his side.

Excitement and anxiety converged uncomfortably. "You found him? Someone?"

"He certainly answers your description," he told her through the opened window. "Tall and lean, white beard, dark face—sells carpets, too. Come and see."

"Is he alone?"

"Shop looks as empty as a robin's nest in winter. He was in the middle of the room tying up a rug, and no customers . . . Come on, we can warn him, carry Ahmad to his cousins and be in Rouida by night."

"Wonderful," she said, and climbed down from the cab. They walked to the souk with its open door, and she stopped on the threshold to look inside. There was a dim anteroom with racks of leather purses and belts but beyond this lay a large room with a skylight that illuminated carpets hanging on the walls in all shapes, sizes, colors and patterns. Under the skylight a bearded man in turban and white djellabah stood examining a small rug; he proceeded to roll it up and when he tucked it under one arm she clearly saw his face and recognized it. Her sense of relief was profound: they would meet with no crisis here, they were home free.

"Yes," she whispered. "Oh thank God yes, he's *just* like his photograph."

"It's Sidi Tahar—it really is?" asked Max, and his voice reflected the same sense of deliverance that she was experiencing.

"Yes." Turning to Ahmad she said, "Wait outside for us, we'll not be long."

He looked anxious. "But *madehm*—"

Max spoke to him in Arabic, and then to her. "I've told him we have business to transact here and he must wait outside."

Ahmad looked sad but he understood authority; he also understood business; he said he would wait outside.

As they entered the souk Sidi Tahar looked up from his work, rose slowly to his feet and began walking toward them, looking very hard at them both, and with such obvious interest that Mrs. Pollifax put a hand to her veil and pulled it aside, smiling and exposing her very American face. "Sidi Tahar Bouseghine," she said.

Max added swiftly, "We're here to say to you *hadha el-husan arej*, the horse is—"

Before Max could complete the words, without any change of expression, Sidi Tahar said in a low voice, "Go, go quickly! Leave at once—flee!"

Astonished, Max said, "But the—"

"Something's wrong, Max," she told him sharply. "Quick, the door—let's go!"

But already it was too late. The anteroom through which they'd entered had not been empty after all; somewhere among its shadows a man had been concealed who emerged now, looking pleased. "So—you are here at last!" he said with the triumphant air of a stalker who has netted his prey.

They had found their imposter but unfortunately he had also found them.

15.
He stood at the edge of the anteroom, a fleecy white djellabah tossed like a shrug over a business suit, a city man very out of place among the carpets and adobe walls, thin-faced with a trim moustache and olive skin. He said, "It has been tiresome waiting for you."

"I beg your pardon!" said Mrs. Pollifax stiffly. It was too late to veil her face again but too soon to entertain the thought of defeat.

His face hardened. "You are the American woman wanted by Security and your name is Pollifax. We know all about you." Reaching under the folds of his djellabah he drew out a pistol, and with the gun in his hand he walked to the door where Ahmad lurked on the threshold. He said curtly, *"Yimshee!* Go away," and slamming the door in his face he slid the bolt across it.

And now Mrs. Pollifax felt the first flicker of fear.

"Oh God," groaned Max.

Sidi Tahar, standing next to her, said gently, "He has been here for three weeks. I'm sorry."

"Yes," she said and added wanly, "We were tired and care-less. And you—has he tried to hurt you?"

He understood. "Only a little," he said in a low voice. "I have been the honey to catch the flies, kept in sight so my neighbors wouldn't wonder at my absence. I did not see why until now, but now . . ."

"Now it's the storage room," said their captor, overhearing his last several words. "To be locked up while I call the police who will be most pleased to end their hunt. You," he said sharply, jabbing a finger at Mrs. Pollifax's chin, "you admit you are the American lady who shot and killed Mr. Max Janko near Erfoud? Confess—this is so, is it not?"

"No it isn't. I didn't kill him, absolutely not," she said truthfully enough.

He snorted indignantly. Turning to Max he said, "And you —who are you? What's your name?"

This was a kinder surprise, his not knowing Max. Trying to look a little stupid Max said, "Bashir Mahbuba," and added a few words in Arabic.

"Yes, but you spoke English before, I heard you," the man said accusingly.

Max shrugged. "English I speak, also French. I give ride to this lady who was in great distress by the road and asks to be lifted to a town. There had been an accident, she said." He added words in French that Mrs. Pollifax didn't understand, inquiring politely at the end, in English, "And your name is—?"

Their captor brushed this aside impatiently. "The name Saleh will do, but I can tell you that this lady's distress is now yours. Come, the souk is closed, we hide you away in another place. Tahar—?" He waved his pistol toward the far end of the shop. "You know the way, open the door."

With a shrug Sidi Tahar walked toward a wall hung with carpets and pushed aside a rug of exquisite symmetry in colors of red, gold, cream and indigo. Behind it lay a door, and when it was opened Mrs. Pollifax saw that it led outside to a short path of sandy soil that ended at a small and windowless hut of adobe. The building sat very precisely behind the souk but it did not stand alone; a cluster of buildings had taken root in the rear of each of the five shops, and around them had sprung up a labyrinth of walls and alleyways.

She thought, *There are three of us and only one of him; if it should be possible—please may it be possible—we could send this man crashing to the ground, we could—* But it was useless to speculate because Saleh maneuvered them with cunning, pressing the gun into the small of her back on the quite accurate assumption that neither of her companions would attempt a rash move that would see her killed.

But really, she thought crossly, *I grow very tired of guns stabbing my back, it begins to be monotonous and it certainly alarms all my spinal discs.*

The door to the hut had an unattractively repressive iron door. After another harsh command Sidi Tahar opened it and the three of them were pushed inside. "Here you stay," Saleh told them. "I call Security, and then—then you will see."

He did not explain what they would see and she was grateful for that because the small dark room into which they'd been shoved was dire enough. It was like a cell, lighted only feebly by a square hole in the ceiling that was covered with an iron grate. The floor was of hardened earth, with a pile of old carpets heaped in the corner, beside which stood a bucket, a clay pitcher, a pillow, a book and a dish.

"You've been kept here?" she asked Sidi Tahar, with a nod at the carpets.

"*Bismallah,* yes. For many nights."

She said with feeling, "While all the time—oh, Sidi Tahar, no one gave a *thought* to your being taken captive and then kept on display in your shop—business as usual—while the imposter hid and waited. Max and I should at least have—" She turned to find Max looking wildly around the room; she said anxiously, "Max?"

He swallowed hard. "I think—I think I've picked up a small case of claustrophobia . . . That damn elevator shaft—" He sank down on the pile of carpets, white and trembling, his head in his hands. "I think I'm going to scream," he said desperately. "I *know* I'm going to scream, I've got to scream, got to . . ."

Sidi Tahar went to him and placed a hand on the nape of his neck. In a soft voice he said, "You must breathe deeply, very long deep breaths, can you do this?"

Mrs. Pollifax stood and watched as Max began an effort to battle his hysteria.

"Now you must close your eyes," said Sidi Tahar calmly. "Close your eyes and picture the desert . . . the desert where space is limitless, the horizon a straight line far, far, far away . . . can you feel it? Perhaps it is the Grand Erg, the sand desert where the shadows are full of color and the sand is golden and there are dunes swept into hills as rounded as the breasts of a woman. The sky overhead is blue and there is freedom—vast freedom—and space," he repeated almost hypnotically. "Space . . . freedom . . . sun . . . sky."

Max jerked once in resistance but at the softness of Sidi Tahar's voice he quieted; she saw his eyelids flicker and his body relax. "There is peace—Allah's peace," murmured Sidi Tahar, watching him intently. Abruptly Max yawned, with a sigh he stretched out on the carpets and closed his eyes and Sidi Tahar removed his hand from his neck.

She looked at him with interest. "Did you hypnotize him, Sidi Tahar?"

He smiled. "I only spoke to the terror in him, gentling it. A memory returned to your friend and became his master, but memory is only illusion. Who is he, by the way? He spoke to me the right words when you entered my souk, but where do you come from, you are both Americans, aren't you? How did you get here? And Saleh spoke of someone dead in Erfoud?"

She sighed. "Does it matter, any of it? How long do we have before the police come, minutes? an hour?"

He said gravely, "I see that you do not know how it is in our mountain villages. Saleh would not approach the gendarmes here, for the local people are my friends and *majlie*. He will have to go to the hotel to use their telephone and call Ourzazate." His eyes smiled at her. "And it would be fortunate if this would be a day the telephone does not connect to the world—this occurs very often. Now speak, tell me who you are and how you happened to walk into my souk today."

She said slowly, "There began to be suspicions in faraway places that something was wrong." She stopped and looked around the room uneasily. "Can we be heard?"

He shook his head. "I have spent many hours here. While Saleh slept on my bed in the souk I read my Koran, meditated, prayed, and grew to know this room very well, because," he explained with a wry smile, "I examined each brick in these walls in hope of getting out to warn friends of what had happened. No, we are not being heard, this I know. You say that somewhere it was understood that something had gone wrong?"

She sighed. "Yes. And it was all so simple at first, I was sent here with seven photographs and addresses to join a Max Janko in Fez, and he and I were to travel down through the country—making no contact, you understand but just making certain that each photo matched the man—and if we found one that didn't we were to cable and call and report this at once."

Puzzled, he said, "But Saleh implied that this man Max Janko has been killed?"

"No," she told him, and pointed to the sleeping Max. *"He's* Max Janko . . . the Janko I met was—oh he was arrogant," she said, remembering. "He insisted I deliver the photos to him and leave, not go with him, and he made me so angry I refused to give the photos to him." She added in surprise, "Which I suppose saved my life. Certainly it turned out to be very fortunate because when his moustache fell off in Erfoud—"

Startled, Sidi Tahar glanced toward Max.

She shook her head. "No, you're looking now at the real one."

"But how—?"

"You heard him speak of an elevator shaft," she said, and she began at the beginning, telling him in detail of her strange journey.

When she had finished Sidi Tahar said simply, "Praise be to Allah, who has preserved you!"

"Yes but Sidi Tahar," she asked, "how did this Saleh learn of you?"

He sighed. "I have thought much on this and I believe it must have happened on the day of the flood six weeks ago, when the Oued Draa was in spate." Seeing her blank look he said, "I speak of the river Draa, which in summer is nearly dry. This year the rains came and the water came rushing down the wadis and there was destruction, but who was to know? I had sent a delivery of carpets to Ourzazate, as was my way, and the young man—a good man, Hafed by name—was to bring back for my souk some carpets made by the Ouzguita tribe. The very smallest carpet I sent with him was to be delivered to a— shall we say a certain person in the marketplace? The name was blessedly not written, but wrapped inside the small carpet was a waterproof package with certain documents and reports."

Sadly he shook his head. "Hafed never reached Ourzazate, he was caught in the flood and was drowned. His truck was returned to his family here in Zagora but the carpets—" He sighed again.

"They were recovered but never returned to you?"

"What else could explain it? It is enough to have lost Hafed, and then suddenly one day neighbors told me questions were being asked about me, and I became aware I was being watched, I made preparations, quite small, to go away for a little while, but that is when Saleh arrived in my souk with his questions and his gun and his threats and—for a little while—the beatings, and he has been here ever since, listening, waiting, calling himself a cousin of mine."

She nodded. "The waterproof package was found, then." When he only shrugged she asked what had to be asked. "And has he made you tell him about our friends in Ourzazate and Rouida?"

His fine eyes examined her without expression. "We have a proverb that says flies do not enter a closed mouth." He said gently, "No, he was told nothing, he could not make me speak. But they are patient, and now—"

She winced. "Now there are three of us." *Three to question,* she thought, *three of us to pressure, interrogate, threaten, harm if necessary,* and remembering Hong Kong she shivered. "The waiting is hard," she admitted.

Sidi Tahar glanced up at the square of light that filtered through the iron rods of the grate. "It is halfway between mid-afternoon and the sunset call to prayer."

"A little after five o'clock," she told him, holding her wrist-watch to the light. "Ourzazate is seventy-five or eighty miles away and that will take time." But they would not come in an ancient truck that climbed the hills slowly, she realized, they would come in fast cars, or perhaps even a helicopter, for undoubtedly they were important enough for the latter if one was available. The news of a network of Polisario informants having been in existence for so long must have proven very humiliating. Heads might already have rolled, and anger and vengeance would surely outweigh moderation.

She remembered Ahmad, and wondered how long he would

wait for them outside before he understood that he'd been abandoned. Would he be able to find his relatives? He'd spoken as if he might have visited them once but it was equally as possible that what he knew had been told him by his father. *At least he knows their name,* she thought wearily, *they can't be too many miles away and perhaps someone will help him.* But it was more probable that he would set out to find his relatives on foot, and her heart ached for him as she pictured him trudging forlornly along the road.

Max's eyes had opened. "I've been listening to you two," he said. "Sidi Tahar, what did you do to me?" He sat up looking cross.

He smiled. "Do you know the meditations of our poet Rumi? He has written that there is no reason for fear, it is our imagination that blocks us just as a wooden bolt holds the door. I loosed the wooden bolt a little, that is all. Perhaps now you can return to the *present* moment."

"Cheerless thought," said Max. "Haven't you noticed we've been very neatly captured and imprisoned?"

"I am not blind," Sidi Tahar told him. "We are in the hands of Allah . . . believe!"

"And if Allah should be blind?"

"Then it would be His will."

Mrs. Pollifax asked with interest, "Are you a mystic, Sidi Tahar, or perhaps a priest?"

Max shook his head. "No by George, he speaks most like a Sufi and I heard him use the word *majlie,* meaning disciple. Are you a Sufi teacher, Sidi Tahar, a darwish or a khalif ar?"

Sidi Tahar shrugged. "These are words, no more."

"A Muslim mystic!" exclaimed Mrs. Pollifax, and with a start of recognition, "But Sufis have also been called whirling dervishes, haven't they? Oh Sidi Tahar, are you a whirling dervish, do you do the dance?"

His eyes smiled at her eagerness. "You mean what we call 'the turning.' It is prayer to us, but a dance, too, you might say —to set one free . . . to climb higher and higher."

"To what?" she asked.

"To Consciousness. To God. To the Light."

"And surely grow dizzy," Max commented dryly.

Curiosity and interest won out over the desolation of her environment. She said, "Could you show me how? Would it be blasphemy to ask it, to ask at least how you whirl and dance?"

He laughed. "And you a *nasrani?* But to amuse you—and is it not a time to forget why?—I will tell you how to begin."

"*Shukren,*" she said, smiling at him.

"Stand," he said.

Max said flippantly, "Easy enough so far."

"Now you must center yourself, the most important part of all." He placed his hand on her solar plexus. "Here is your center. Feel it. Without a center there is no turning, no dance."

Mrs. Pollifax placed her hand there and waited.

"Now to receive your first lesson, cross your arms, your right hand on your left shoulder, the left hand on the right shoulder." He nodded. "And turn counter-clockwise but slowly, first to your left and then, round and round."

With arms crossed she turned, managing it only twice before dizziness overcame her and she stopped. Sidi Tahar smiled. "You were not centered. Try again but this time you will turn without your left foot leaving the floor."

She stared at him in astonishment. "Without my left foot— but that's impossible!"

He laughed. "You pick up your right foot and you put it down on the other side of the leg, and you turn. And you turn without moving the left foot, as if it is nailed to the floor. In fact in the old days a big nail would be driven into the floor

149

between the toes of the left foot so that it could never leave the earth."

Mrs. Pollifax tried this, clumsily turned and collapsed on the carpet beside Max. When she had caught her breath she smiled at Sidi Tahar. "There is more to this than I believed!"

"There is more to everything than one believes," he said. "The 'turning,' the whirling, takes one to the still point of the universe, and how can *that* be easily learned?"

Beside her Max said in a burst of anger, "This is ridiculous, damn it, don't you realize that we've got to think what to do and say? We've got to plan, get our stories straight . . . The police could come at any minute and my God, you're taking lessons in dancing?"

She looked at Sidi Tahar and smiled. "You don't understand, Max, he'd never share this under any other circumstances, he's trying to distract us."

Max pointed to the grate in the roof. "That's all very well but can't you see how dark it's getting? It doesn't give us much time to plan."

Sidi Tahar frowned. "It can't be dark yet, the muezzin has not begun the sunset call to prayer."

What Sidi Tahar said was true; even Mrs. Pollifax's wristwatch told her that it couldn't be sunset yet. Puzzled, she rose and walked to the center of the room to stare up at the hole in the ceiling that had lost its daylight. Standing there she said, "Someone has covered up the grate." She felt something tickle her nose and brushed it impatiently aside but a second later it returned to tickle her cheek. Assuming it to be a cobweb she reached out to grasp it this time and discovered that it was not a cobweb but a string. "Look!" she gasped. "A string!" Lifting her head she exclaimed, "Someone must be up there lying across the grate, which is why it's dark!"

They moved to examine her discovery. Running the string

through her fingers she said, "And look—feel—there's a *pebble* attached to the end of it." Excitedly she said, "Max, it has to be Ahmad, who else could it be? He must still be in Zagora and is trying to help!"

Max grasped the string, his fingers following it until he reached the pebble at its end. "It's certainly attached to something or someone up above—and look, there's more than a pebble here, there's a scrap of paper tied to the pebble. Have we a match?"

Sidi Tahar brought them his candle and lighted it, and now there was no question about it: someone on the roof had sent them a message. Mrs. Pollifax opened up the wad of paper to find two childlike drawings in pencil. In the flickering candlelight they peered at the scrap of paper, frowning over what looked like the drawing of a key, and below it a second primitive sketch of two circles set into a box.

Pointing to the latter Max said, "That's a truck, it has to be, and those are wheels."

"The other looks like a key," contributed Mrs. Pollifax. "What's the swirl of Arabic writing at the bottom?"

Max said excitedly, "It really is from Ahmad, he's signed his name. You're right—he's here, he found us and he's on the roof."

Mrs. Pollifax sent him a silent thank you, her heart warmed by the thought of his presence. "I think he wants us to send up the key to the truck."

Max looked at her in horror. "But why? We mustn't!"

Mrs. Pollifax said indignantly, "What do you mean *'mustn't'*?"

"If we ever get out of here the truck's our only hope. Why would he want the key, does he plan to sell the truck for money?"

" 'O ye of little faith,' " chided Mrs. Pollifax. "If he can use money as a bribe to get us out, send up the key to him."

"Damn it, he's only nine years old."

"The truck is scarcely of any use to us here, Max," she said tartly. "Don't underestimate Ahmad, he's a clever little boy. Send him up the key."

"But do you really think it wise?"

"You might consider the alternative," she told him dryly.

Max sighed. "Well, he's certainly been loyal to have stuck around like this, unless of course they're holding a gun on him up there to make him do this."

She sniffed. "I'd no idea you suffered from paranoia, Max."

"You won't accept the wrecked nerves of a claustrophobic?"

She said impatiently, "If Saleh has found our truck and wants the key, need I point out that he would only walk in that door and take it from you?"

"You have a point," he admitted generously. "Obviously I'm falling apart in this hellhole. Sidi Tahar—?"

Sidi Tahar laughed. "Ali the Lion, caliph of Islam, has spoken of three things that can never be retrieved, the last of which is a missed opportunity."

"I won't ask what the others are," said Max. "Okay, let's see if opportunity knocks." He brought the key from his pocket and carefully tied it to the end of the string, gave it a tug, and it vanished from his grasp into the darkness. They knew that it reached the grate when the silhouette of a hand appeared and guided the key between the bars. Following this both the hand and the shadow disappeared, and daylight shone again through the hole.

"So much for that," Max said grimly. "Our entertainment for this hour. What do you think will happen next?"

"What happens next," said Sidi Tahar tranquilly, "is already written."

Mrs. Pollifax responded to the serenity in his voice and relaxed. "We must strike you as very impatient."

"Possibly Europeans are," he said. "And Americans. There is a story of a King who summoned all his wise men to his palace and promised a rich reward to the one who could sum up for him in just one sentence all the wisdom of living, just one sentence that would contribute to every possible event in a lifetime."

"And?" asked Mrs. Pollifax, smiling.

Sidi Tahar chuckled. "The wisest of them wrote for him just four words: *This too shall pass.* And so it is with the three of us crouched in this dark room: this too shall pass."

"It will pass, yes," grumbled Max, "but how? Remember, the police can still come at any minute and take us away, or even worse we could be—"

"Such words!" interrupted Sidi Tahar with a shake of his head. "They stab, they disturb the peace of the heart! Try to be calm—be in the world but not of it!"

Max subsided but Mrs. Pollifax could feel his claustrophobic panic growing again and accumulating a life of its own until it felt like a fourth person occupying the room with them. She hoped he would remain silent now. Their prospects, his and hers, were not rosy but were somewhat improved by their being foreigners. It was Sidi Tahar whose future was anything but promising—after all, he was a native of this country and therefore could be called a traitor; it was kinder not to think what awaited him. She thought instead about Ahmad and of how so very little kindness had won such a staunch loyalty from him; she felt again the touch of his confiding hand in hers and visualized the radiance of his sudden smile, and then she thought of Cyrus, still in Kenya and assuming that she was safely at home. Whatever lay ahead for her would not be easy; she was known to have set out from Fez with the false Max Janko, and he was now dead. She would be accused, no doubt, of his murder and there would be no help from Carstairs, that was always part of the bargain, but in this case she would feel especially compelled to protect him from his own people. She owed him that. "Maverick department, Atlas—very secret," Bishop had explained.

No, there would be no help from Langley, Virginia, nor would she ask for it. It might even be wise of her to confess to Flavien's murder herself, for if Max hadn't shot him she would certainly have done her best to kill him, and didn't the thought equal the deed? As a woman and an American she might be treated a shade more gently than Max, who was very obviously connected with the CIA, having been Flavien's boss in Cairo.

They would know things like that.

No, she thought sadly, Cyrus would *not* find her waiting for him when he came home, and how naively she'd believed that she would be back among her geraniums by that date! A week's jaunt through Morocco, Bishop had told her—and here she was in a dark mountain village in the south of Morocco, captive and without hope of deliverance.

She leaned her head back against the wall and for a moment or two closed her eyes. When she opened them it was to see that Sidi Tahar, seated on the earth floor, was watching her. He smiled. In his craggy dark face his smile was beautiful and she smiled back. She had met with a Sufi; now she asked, "Are you also a prophet, Sidi Tahar?"

His smile deepened and his eyes twinkled. "We have an ancient story about that, a joke if you will . . . There was once a man who announced himself a prophet on arrival in a strange village, and the townspeople asked, 'What are the proofs of your being a prophet?' And he said, 'The proof I offer is to tell you exactly what is in your minds.' They said eagerly, 'Tell us, then, what do you see in our minds?' And he replied, 'You are thinking that I am a liar and not a prophet at all.' "

She laughed. "I like your stories and your proverbs. Tell me, where did you learn to speak such excellent English?"

"During the Second World War," he said. "I left Morocco to fight with the Free French, and spent a few years with English and Americans fighting in North Africa."

"Hey," said Max from his corner.

She nodded. "Yes!" And leaning forward she said to him, "And did you save a man's life in Tripoli, Sidi Tahar?"

He smiled. "So you *do* know Carstairs."

"Yes, it's he who sent me. And because in a way he saved *my* life," she told him gravely, "I thank you for saving his."

"Some men are like good bread, others like stones," he said. "How could one abandon such a man?"

From beyond the walls there came to them now the call of the muezzin to prayer, to the *shehada,* the ululating voice rising and falling . . . The time of sunset had arrived. Sidi Tahar sank to the floor and touched the ground with his forehead, intoning *"la ilah Allah wa—Muhammed rasul Allah. . . .* !"

She closed her eyes, listening and hoping to exorcise the growing tension of waiting.

◎

16. *Mornajay* judged it to be a three-hour drive
from Marrakech to the Tizi Pass and he drove as fast as hills and traffic permitted, wanting to cross the pass before any new snows intervened, and in time to reach Ourzazate for a very

late dinner. He admitted to a sense of exhilaration at what lay ahead of him: Tizi-n-Tichka was the highest peak in the long line of the High Atlas range, the pass itself 7414 feet high, and this was January. He was leaving behind a temperate zone of heavily fruited orange trees, bougainvillea, fertile gardens and villages, and for contrast he need only glance skyward to see ahead of him the towering snow-frosted mountains. From his college days he remembered that Pliny had written of a Roman named Suetonius Paulinus who had crossed the High Atlas at Tizi Pass in the fifth century. *My God, how long ago,* he thought; it was exciting to think of a Roman traveler daring such a journey for in those days not many people ventured far from the coast of the Mediterranean. On the ancient maps of the region the Maghreb had been called Mauritania, which had nothing to do with the present country of that name in the south, and from this region the Romans had extracted fruit, grain, animals and gold but most of all slaves, in fact once on the other side of the mountains he would meet the old caravan routes that had crossed the Sahara to trade and sell in Fez for centuries.

He drove past sunny green fields, men astride donkeys hung with panniers, and then the town of Ait-Ourir, and following this the traffic thinned. Soon he began his ascent into the mountains. The road was narrow and winding but it had been cleared, leaving snow in great piles on either side. As he rounded one long curve he was surprised to see a small espresso cafe clinging to the sides of the cliff out of which the road was carved, and having met with no traffic at all he decided to stop and inquire about conditions ahead.

In the deserted cafe a gnarled little old man sat behind the counter, the usual fading photograph of the King framed on the wall behind him. A few tables and chairs were scattered around the room, and through the windows Mornajay saw that a broad wooden deck had been built outside to hold more tables.

"*Bonjour,*" said Mornajay. "*Une espresso.*"

"*Une espresso,*" said the man, nodding, and to Mornajay's questions he replied that, yes, the Pass had been closed for some hours the day before but by noon it had been opened to one-way traffic, and today traffic was normal and the roads cleared all the way.

Even as he said this a truck could be heard shifting gears as it passed the cafe and headed down toward Marrakech.

Mornajay nodded and thanked him. Carrying his espresso he strolled out onto the deck and stopped in astonishment, spellbound. Far far below him, perhaps half a mile under the cafe, lay a fertile valley of green fields with a cluster of tiny houses tucked into its folds, but what equally amazed him was that the green fields had been built into terraces that seemed to flow up the mountain to where he stood and beyond him, terrace after terrace rising like stairs out of that deep valley until it met the snow line where only rock endured, and above that—he flung back his head to look—it met with craggy peaks and blue sky.

He felt taken out of himself . . . The silence was profound, the sun was warm on his face, the air tart and crisp. He looked again into the valley hidden below the wall of mountain and he thought, "Here is Shangri-la, I must come back to this one day."

He wouldn't, of course, and he knew it, nor was there any need to return, it was simply one of those unexpected moments that engraved itself upon a person's soul and he was grateful to be touched by it. For so many years of his adult life he'd been an obsessed man, sternly protecting himself against emotion, but during the past year—trying to learn again how to live—he'd begun to understand how impoverished and empty he'd become. This moment filled him, and that was enough.

He lingered a few more minutes, both the espresso and the sun warming him, his eyes softening as he dreamed over the peaceful scene, and then with a sigh he remembered why he was here on his way to Ourzazate and went back to his car.

It was at some point following the descent from Tizi Pass and during the long drive through a wasteland of rust-colored escarpments and hills that Mornajay wondered if it might not be sensible for him to look up the agent whom Bartlett had told him was in Ourzazate. Jenkins was the man's name, he remembered, and he could be found at the Hotel Raid Salaam. He'd not seriously considered doing this earlier but the deeper he traveled into this country the more incredible he found it that Mrs. Pollifax could have evaded the police for this long. He'd told Carstairs on the phone that it would be similar to looking for a needle in a haystack but as he digested the total emptiness of the landscape through which he passed he realized that any Westerner—and a woman at that—would be so conspicuous as to change this analogy completely: It was much more like looking for a haystack in a field of needles.

Her disappearance seemed so inconceivable that he felt he should stop to see Jenkins and discover if she'd been found by now.

He tried to think back to the Mrs. Pollifax he'd known at such a crucial time in Thailand. This was difficult for him to do because he'd been a different person then, totally occupied with his own secret mission; he'd been irritable and impatient at every obstacle he'd met, and Mrs. Pollifax had been one of them. His earliest impression of her had been that she was a fool, and—he smiled faintly—that she'd been determined to insult him. Yet when he'd lain in the jungle half out of his head with fever and hallucinations she'd not deserted him and it was because of her and her Thai companion that he was alive today. He'd been able to repay her later by helping her and her husband but he'd never been curious about her presence in such wild country. Knowing now who she was, and what she was, he looked back on the experience with a different eye. What he had taken as insults from her, he admitted wryly, was merely bluntness: she had been as irritated and as impatient with him as he had been with her, and recalling his pompousness he winced. If she'd been capable of saving his life, and her husband's, then she was quite capable of preserving her own life, but *how*, he wondered, and where was she, and what would she do? In Thailand she'd kept a cool head, she'd had resolution, stamina and resourcefulness. Was she holed up somewhere in hiding, or on the move . . . ?

He thought, *What would I do in her situation?*

He thought, *In the country of the blind I would pretend to be blind.*

"Aha!" he cried aloud triumphantly. "Exactly!" And he smiled.

He knew what he assumed no one else knew, and this was the last name on the list that Mrs. Pollifax had been given, which was that of Khaddour Nasiri in the village of Rouida. If she was caught before she reached that village—if she was found hiding in Erfoud, or making her way to Ourzazate or Zagora—he knew there was absolutely nothing he could do for her, the pursuit was too organized.

But if by chance or luck she succeeded in reaching Rouida there was a great deal that he could do for her.

He would not stop in Ourzazate after all, he would head directly for Rouida.

Drawing up to the side of the road he stopped the car and brought out his wallet. From an assortment of forged identification papers and passports he selected a press card with his photo and the name of Ambrose Cunningham. This and his camera should suffice to get him a laissez-passer that would see him through the military roadblock on the way to Rouida. His guidebook did not mention why traffic on the road to Rouida had to be stopped and inspected but it needed only a glance at a map to understand why: the village lay a scant forty miles from the Algerian border.

He felt elated by his decision, reckless as it might prove. To hell with Ourzazate and Jenkins, he thought, he would secure the necessary laissez-passer in Zagora and then head directly to Rouida as Ambrose Cunningham, photographer for a major news magazine in search of desert exotica.

17.

In Zagora Mrs. Pollifax had fallen asleep when Max nudged her, saying in a low voice, "Listen!" and to Sidi Tahar, "Are you hearing something, too?"

Beyond the flickering candle Sidi Tahar leaned forward and whispered back, "I hear. There are sounds from outside, behind the wall next me, the back wall."

Mrs. Pollifax, listening and frowning, said, "It sounds like a car with its motor running. What could it be?"

"But it doesn't stop," pointed out Max. "A car ought to drive away, and if it's the police they'd surely go to the souk and come through the door over *there*."

Sidi Tahar leaned close to the wall to listen. "It is not going away, it is very near—inches near."

Mrs. Pollifax, thoroughly awake now, rose to her feet.

"That's not a car," she said, "it sounds more like—Max, I believe it's a *truck*."

Max said incredulously, "But how, what—what's it doing? And why is it there?"

The sound of the engine outside suddenly accelerated, no longer idling but rising in sound, and as it grew louder they moved to the middle of the room and stood together, tense and wondering, vaguely threatened and deeply curious.

"*Look!*" cried Sidi Tahar and pointed at the wall, which had begun to tremble, as if under great pressure.

An adobe brick dropped away to the earth and then another. Abruptly the sound of the engine turned into a great roar and more bricks toppled, dust rose in clouds and the nose of a truck edged its way into the room and stopped. It was their Volvo, and seated behind the wheel, scarcely discernible, sat a very small Ahmad. Even in the dim light they could see his huge proud smile.

"*Bisura, bisura,*" urged Ahmad, leaning out of the window. "Please—I do not know how to send it back."

Max raced for the driver's seat and Mrs. Pollifax and Sidi Tahar followed, stumbling over fallen bricks to climb in beside him, where Sidi Tahar lifted Ahmad to his lap. Max shifted gears into reverse; the truck protested, shuddered and moved a few inches, sending a rain of fresh bricks down on the roof of the cab, and then stalled, ominously. Desperately Max pressed the accelerator to the floor, the engine returned to life and the truck slowly inched its way out of the ragged, gaping hole that its ramming had created. Once outside and free of debris it then became necessary to continue backing down a long narrow alley with buildings on either side. With relief they emerged at last into a broad dirt road that serviced the cluster of huts around the souks.

"Wphew," gasped Max. "Tight squeeze . . . All right, Sidi

Tahar, now where, is there a way to avoid the road to the hotel?"

Sidi Tahar pointed. "Turn left, this trail leads behind hill and hotel to exit on the highway south."

"Thank God," murmured Max. "That road to the hotel is a dead-end death trap. Ahmad, you okay?"

Ahmad was still beaming. "Oh . . . *kay,*" he said with delight.

The truck had lost one of its headlights from the ramming and the trail was no more than a cart-path; they bumped over rocks and swerved around trees, knowing they were now in a race for their lives. The town looked to be asleep, there were no lights showing except at the hotel, but if Saleh had not heard the crashing of bricks behind the souk there were sure to be neighbors who would rush to speak of the strange truck that had made such a hole in the storage hut. After so many hours of waiting for the police their arrival must be imminent, too; they might even be drawing up to the front door of the souk as they escaped from the rear . . .

Realizing the miracle of this escape Mrs. Pollifax leaned over and kissed Ahmad on the top of his head.

Sidi Tahar, nodding to her, said, "He has *baraka*, this boy."

"What's that?"

"The benediction of Allah. I would like to instruct such a boy."

She gave him a quick glance at this but there was no time for response for they had just gained the paved highway. Max braked, and four heads swivelled right and then left to observe the dark road. Finding it empty of traffic Max turned south. "Now we look for Ahmad's aunt," he said and added grimly, "and try to make plans for ourselves after that. Sidi Tahar, you know this part of the country, you're in this mess too, where and how do we—"

"Later," he said calmly. "Our fates are joined together—I too am thinking. One matter at a time."

"Where are the directions to Ahmad's cousins?" Mrs. Pollifax asked.

Digging in his pocket Max handed a slip of paper to her without looking at her. "I wrote them in English. It shouldn't be far, only about five miles Muhammed said . . . something about a cemetery and a road beyond it. Still have your pocket flashlight?"

In its thin beam of light she read out the words he'd scribbled down in Ourzazate. "About five miles out of Zagora a cemetery on right side of road, bordered on south by line of olive trees. Just beyond trees a dirt road. Turn down it—one mile to village."

Max said, "With only one headlight it's going to need four pairs of eyes to find that cemetery."

She nodded but she knew what to look for now: here in the south the graveyards were very different from those she'd seen in the north. At first casual glance they looked like a field of broken shards; it needed a second glance to see how the jagged points of broken flagstones had been pressed into the earth in neat rows, one at the head of the grave, another at the foot, the graves very close together. They had reminded her of the pretend-gardens that she'd made as a child by sticking twigs and stones into the earth. They were the graves of a people who lived in a harsh poor land, they were desert graves.

"Yes it will be hard to find in the darkness," she agreed, and to Ahmad, "We must look closely, Ahmad."

Max said irritably, "I feel conspicuous, we can be seen for miles, damn it, even with only one headlight. What do we do if a car comes?"

"Pray," said Mrs. Pollifax.

"*Bismallah*," contributed Sidi Tahar.

A sliver of moon was rising in the east, the mountains black against a night sky of indigo blue dusted with stars. No lights could be seen anywhere at all in the great sweep of countryside that surrounded them. Her wristwatch told her that it was half-past nine but if there were any householders in the valley they had all retired for the night. "There!" cried Ahmad, and she saw it, too: a straight line of trees ahead, and soon the solitary beam of headlight picked out the broken stones of the graveyard. "At last," she breathed.

Max slowed the truck, they passed the trees, and there was the road, deeply rutted, its spine as broken as the flagstones in the cemetery. Max growled, "This has to be the coup de grace for our shock absorbers, it has to be."

She said tartly, "I didn't know we had any." They bumped over holes and hillocks, heading across a barren plain with only a few tufts of grass and scrub visible, and then Mrs. Pollifax saw a whitewashed dome and a row of adobe houses pressed against a hill. It was difficult to think of this as a village, and perhaps it wasn't, but they had arrived.

Ahmad said comfortably, "*There* is the house of my mother's sister." He pointed.

Max did not drive up to the house but headed around it to hide the truck in the rear. A dog barked. A dim light suddenly appeared in the house, they had been heard, and as they climbed down from the cab a door opened and a man with a lantern peered out, the light shining on a white shirt that reached his ankles.

"'Amm Mahfoud!" cried Ahmad joyously, racing toward him.

"Ahmad?" faltered the man, and as he lifted his lantern Mrs. Pollifax saw a worn dark face with a gray beard. Ahmad erupted into words, none of which Mrs. Pollifax could understand, and touching her arm Max said, "I have the distinct feeling that no one speaks English, which is going to be damnably boring for you but I'll do my best to keep you informed."

"Thank you," she said. "I can already guess what Ahmad's telling him because he's quickly snuffed out his lantern."

"So he has," said Max, and they moved toward the two figures on the threshold.

Sidi Tahar, following tranquilly behind them, paused to bow and say, "Salam Alaikum."

Startled, Ahmad's uncle said, "Alaikum wa Salam," and then, peering at him more closely, "You are the holy man from Zagora!" And with a bow he touched his heart with his hand and bid them come inside.

They sat on pillows in the house of Mahfoud. A single candle had been lighted, but not until both window and door had been well sheathed against the glow of its light. While the others talked earnestly and with passion in their own language Mrs. Pollifax looked around her with curiosity: this was her first glimpse into the interior of a real home. She was seeing a long room with whitewashed walls, along which lay bright pillows and carpets for sleeping and sitting, and a few small low tables. The earth floor was covered with reed mats. In the corner a young boy still slept soundly, a dark shape that turned restlessly but did not awaken. An older boy, in his teens, had roused and sat watching them silently. Nearby, Mahfoud's wife was ladling soup from a kettle into four bowls, turning from moment to moment when she heard something startling, her glance sliding to Mrs. Pollifax before she returned to the food. The soup would be cold, Max had told her in an aside, they did not dare a fire to heat it but it was *harira* soup and would be delicious.

She decided that she would like some delicious soup very much, whether it was hot or cold, having eaten no food since breakfast. This was a moment when she was content to let all the strange words flow past her without understanding any of them, or knowing what plans were being discussed. The police had to be looking for them and for the truck by now. It was doubtful they could stay long here when a thorough search would eventually bring the police to this out-of-the-way hamlet and endanger Ahmad's relatives. She would therefore exist only in this hour; she would rest, not worry, not consider the next hour, which looked dark and possibly dangerous, she would let Max and Sidi Tahar argue possibilities without querying them.

Max turned to her abruptly. "Both Sidi Tahar and Mahfoud tell me there is a checkpoint between here and Rouida, about four miles from here. Not for us," he added quickly, "it's always there, one needs a pass to get through because Rouida is close to the border."

Mahfoud's wife brought her soup and a spoon, giving her a faint smile. "*Shurba,*" she said, and went back to carry soup to Ahmad, who sat cross-legged on the floor following the conversation with huge eyes.

Again Max turned to her. "Mahfoud calls it twenty-five miles in distance from this house to Rouida. We can't stay, of course, we've got to leave. I've asked for his help and offered him the truck in return, it's all we have to give him and it's of no use to us any farther. He tells me—"

He means we must walk, she realized.

"—tells me he accepts the truck with deep thanks but it mustn't be found here. His older son Rashid will drive us into the hills as far as possible and then hide the truck in a wadi or cave. After this Rashid will leave us, knowing exactly where the truck is hidden, and—"

"And we walk," she said, sparing him the word, knowing that of course it was the only way for them to get past any checkpoint and reach Rouida without being seen. Valleys were nicely flat but inhabited. Only mountains could conceal them now but she did hope they were not *high* mountains, for if they had looked like mesas framed against the night sky they were surely steep. She tried not to think of this; after all they had little choice in this attempt to reach Khaddour Nasiri in Rouida, and if they reached him she could only hope he would be trustworthy and know what to do with two *nasrani* and a Sufi on the run.

They were talking again but she could no longer relax now that Max had begun directing small shocks at her. She began to apply herself to the soup, which was as delicious as Max had said it would be.

Suddenly Mahfoud blew out the candle and hushed them. He walked to the window, tugged at the blanket over it and peered outside. They waited in silence, listening, and then Mrs. Pollifax heard it, too, the sound of cars or trucks a mile away on the highway. Until now she had not realized the utter silence in a country village at night, or how sound traveled in such silence. Now she, too, waited to learn whether the sounds faded or turned toward them to grow louder.

The sounds grew softer, faded and disappeared and the room was filled with sighs of relief. Mahfoud hung the blanket over the window but he didn't light the candle again and when he spoke his voice was agitated. He was afraid, and Mrs. Pollifax, guessing his thoughts, lifted her bowl to her lips to empty it before they were told to leave.

She had not been entirely correct, however, because now the name of Ahmad was repeated a number of times, and she could see him squirming where he sat. Sidi Tahar spoke, Ahmad spoke, Mahfoud's wife broke in and then Mahfoud. "What is it, Max?" she interrupted.

"They are saying now that Ahmad should go with us. They

know Sidi Tahar is a holy man because he has the mark—the *sudjda*—on his forehead from his devotions. They trust him. They don't say they know where Sidi Tahar is going, but they tell me that if his parents come for Ahmad they would only take him where Sidi Tahar is going, and it would be safer for him to go with us."

"Safer? I wish I could share their faith," she said ruefully. "Do they know we're being hunted, dreadful word?"

"Well yes," Max said, "but you see—" He shrugged help-lessly, with a smile. "They're not terribly interested in us, we're only *nasrani*, but Sidi Tahar is a holy man." He lowered his voice to a near whisper. "What they suggest makes me think they know a great deal more than we give them credit for, and they're very doubtful that Ahmad will ever see his parents again."

"Oh no," she protested, and then stifled her obvious words of alarm and said weakly, "Insh'Allah," understanding that this was no moment to worry over Ahmad's parents when there were so many other worries. They must get away quickly now, before any cars turned down the dirt road by the graveyard to search for them here. There was the walk into the hills that lay ahead of them, too, but the important thing was to *go*.

The talk had ended, and Max and Sidi Tahar were rising. She carried her empty soup bowl to Mahfoud's wife and thanked her. They walked out of the house to the truck, led this time by Mahfoud's son Rashid who would drive now, with Max seated in the cab beside him.

There was a flurry of farewells, punctuated by Bismallahs and Insh'Allahs; Mrs. Pollifax and Sidi Tahar and Ahmad were helped into the open back of the truck, and with a grinding of gears they pulled away, heading now across untilled ground and over roadless fields toward the rocky hills they hoped would conceal them.

18.

Mornajay approached Rouida in mid-afternoon of the next day, stopping his car on the outskirts to observe it and guess what he might expect. Off to his far right the last of the mesas had dropped away until it was no more than a *djebal* of rocks pointing a finger to the south. Ahead of him sprawled the village, and beyond it he saw with great pleasure that he had reached the true desert at last: it stretched without interruption as far as the eye could see, a seemingly unending flow of sand and pebble that met with nothing at all until it reached the distant horizon and a cerulean blue sky. He'd forgotten what such space could be like, and how it rested a man. Even the village, its adobe built from the same desert sand, matched it in color, blended into it and merged with only the shadows cast by the sun defining its difference, the sun-baked walls blank except for the occasional small square window or the longer shadows of mysterious entrances.

He wondered at Rouida's taking root here in this inhospitable corner of the country, and then in the foreground he saw the well, circled by concrete, and this clearly explained the reason for its fragile existence at the fringe of the desert: there was water here, it was an oasis. Not one of Hollywood's lush date-palm oases, for he saw only one tree rising above the low flat roofs, and it was this deficiency that gave the village the look of bones that had been stripped and bleached by the sun. There were no roads or streets; compounds stood apart with great spaces between them, as if to give release to the inhabitants from the narrow alleys and dark rooms inside. If there was wealth here, he thought, it was well hidden from the tax-collectors. There were certainly no shops for tourists but a long low building bore a cola sign in faded colors: this shabby cafe and the well, then, marked the center of Rouida and this was substantiated by the several groups of men who stood talking or idling under the cola sign.

In Zagora he had visited the prefecture to receive his laissez-passer to travel here. The man had made every attempt to send a Tuareg guide with him but Mornajay had frostily argued him down, emphasizing his press card, dramatically holding up his camera and repeating over and over that he needed to spend more than an hour in Rouida.

"It is already past noon," the prefecture had pointed out.

He had agreed that yes, it was indeed early afternoon.

"There are no hotels or hostels for the night," the Prefect had emphasized.

Mornajay had replied that he was quite capable of sleeping in his car.

Why was this?

"Because," Mornajay had explained, "I wish to photograph the desert at sunset and at dawn, being *not* a tourist but a photographer, a man of work."

Reluctantly he had been given his pass, which he would soon have to present to the prefecture here to be stamped—whatever came to Rouida must also leave Rouida, he thought wryly. He would then have to find and introduce himself to the headman of the village if he was to breach those inhospitable blank walls facing him. He drew out the list that Carstairs had read to him over the phone in Spain and reassured himself that it was Khaddour Nasiri, the bathhouse keeper, for whom he must look. He nodded; a public bath was an excellent place for hearing gossip and news; certainly anyone riding into Rouida from the desert along the caravan trails from Mali, Mauritania or even, furtively, from Algeria, would almost immediately head for the bathhouse to wash away the heat and grit of the desert . . . and to talk.

But there were no clues as to where the bathhouse was located. Beyond the cafe he could see the flat-roofed squares of compounds extending out into the desert—urban sprawl, he thought wryly—and he was reasonably certain, given the architecture of the country, that a maze of alleyways and narrow passages lay behind each of those blank closed walls, as well as dozens of families.

He would need to be persuasive and very, very careful. Challenged by the uncertainties that lay ahead he pressed his foot to the accelerator and drove into Rouida.

The headman of the village was named Madani el-Kebaj, and he proved to be a mixture of centuries of intermarriage among the desert tribes. His royal bearing suggested Tuareg blood but his Sudanese heritage had given him a polished black face that was dramatically framed by a snowy white turban. He wore a gray djellabah, and thrust into his broad leather belt was a genuinely old and extraordinary knife with intricate silver designs. Speaking in French Mornajay introduced himself, presented his laissez-passer and his ID card to him, and watched as he read both of them carefully with pursed lips. When the man spoke it was in a surprisingly soft, almost caressing voice, and in English. "Please allow me to offer you tea."

Mornajay smiled politely and with effusive thanks asked if he might first take photographs while the light was so fine, and accept el-Kebaj's invitation at a later hour. "I'd like to catch some of the normal life here in your town. Its being at the edge of the desert"—he gestured toward the golden brown sand that stretched to the horizon—"makes it of special interest."

"Yes? Such as what?" he was asked curiously.

"The *ferran*—public ovens—perhaps? and the bathhouse? and perhaps—" He shrugged. "Are there camels about?"

El-Kebaj said helpfully, "We expect a caravan in the morning."

"Wonderful," Mornajay told him. *"Bon!* I've been given the okay to stay for two days, a pity its not longer but that's why I'd like to start at once if you don't mind."

El-Kebaj gravely bowed. "I offer you the hospitality of my house, then, for the night."

"Very kind," Mornajay said uneasily. "Very kind indeed. Now I wonder if you could show me just where the bread is made, and where the baths are, and—" He was beginning to feel foolish, "—I imagine you have splendid sunsets, I'll want to capture one of those."

The djellabah rustled, el-Kebaj nodded and he was led past the cafe and around the corner into the great open sandy space that separated the walled compounds. *Of course,* he thought, *these great spaces are a necessity for camel caravans . . . try herding hundreds of camels into a narrow alleyway!* The sun was warm but not searing. They passed an archway leading into a narrow alley and then some distance beyond it an open door, and here el-Kebaj slowed his pace.

"The hammam," he said, pointing.

"The what?"

"Bathhouse. Behind it, against its other wall, is the public oven. It will be hot, monsieur, we will go in."

It was a very efficient combination, thought Mornajay, a huge open oven, flames leaping upward—to the right the entrance to the women's bathhouse, to the left the men's—and presumably the baker of bread drew from the same fire in the rear. It would make sense, of course, with fuel being so scarce . . . A boy was tending the fire, an older man haranguing him. He was swarthy, with a bristling moustache, and if this was the bathhouse keeper he wondered how to get the man alone and talk to him.

"His name?" he asked politely, inserting a flashbulb into his camera.

"Khaddour Nasiri," explained the headman.

Mornajay lifted the camera to his eye and snapped a photograph. Hearing his name spoken Nasiri turned and looked grumpily at Mornajay and managed a reluctant nod. "Do you speak French?" asked Mornajay.

Nasiri shrugged indifferently. *"Oui."*

"One more picture and then I wonder if I could photograph you outside in the light, with the building behind you . . . Could you spare a minute?"

El-Kebaj gave the man a nod, suggesting that he do this, and Mornajay realized the headman was going to accompany them, that in this village where nothing much happened he was providing the headman with an Event. He should have guessed this; with a sigh he led them out, where the two men stood uncertainly in the sun and a swarm of boys came running. It was ironic, it was comical and it was terrible, there was to be no privacy at all.

Orders were issued by el-Kebaj and the boys stood back, chattering among themselves, giggling—a wretched lot, thought Mornajay testily, and they'd soon be begging money from him. He posed Khaddour Nasiri alone in front of the door in the wall and drew back to join the headman and the boys and focus his camera.

He found his problem not insoluble. With everyone watching and waiting he suddenly grunted, shook his head in dismay and walked up to Nasiri to fuss with his turban. Arranging it more artistically he murmured in a low voice, "I must speak with you alone, Khaddour Nasiri. There has been trouble. If I mention the names of Sidi Tahar Bouseghine in Zagora and Muhammed Tuhami in Ourzazate you will believe?"

Nasiri turned his head to look at him but his expression remained unchanged. Mornajay withdrew to begin snapping photos, kneeling, standing, turning to include the headman and the children. Presently, with this scene exhausted, he handed out one-dirham coins until his pockets were empty, thanked el-Kebaj, and begged to be left alone to wander around taking a few photographs at random. The headman hesitated and then nodded, spoke harshly to the boys, gesturing them away, and promised tea when Mornajay was finished.

Relieved of both headman and boys, Mornajay turned and strolled casually up the broad and sandy thoroughfare past the last mud-stained walls of the village toward the greater open space beyond that was peopleless and flat and almost golden in the late afternoon sun: the desert.

He felt Khaddour Nasiri's approach before he was joined by him.

"There is trouble?" said Nasiri softly, standing beside him.

"There is trouble," Mornajay told him. "If your Allah is kind they may come to Rouida. There is no longer any other way out of the country and the police are looking for them."

" 'They?' " he repeated alertly, a different Nasiri now.

Mornajay nodded. "Yes, and we must pray for baraka. Two people, one of them a woman, came from the West knowing something was wrong. Now everything is wrong, they too are in trouble and 'on the run,' if you know what that means. Have you any transport?"

"A very old truck with old tires," said Nasiri, nodding, and added with a faint smile, "but the engine is fine and new, and there are big desert tires safely hidden away. A wireless is also hidden."

Mornajay snapped a picture of the empty desert and then

turned to Nasiri, smiled at him and lifted his camera to film a close-up of his head. "Get them ready," he said out of the corner of his mouth. "And it might be wise to find a turban and djellabah, very old and worn, for me." With a final nod he strolled on toward the desert to take several more photographs. When he turned back Nasiri was gone.

Unfortunately his feeling of success—after all, he had reached Rouida and found Khaddour Nasiri, which was no small job—began to dissipate during the next hour when he was given too much time to think. He had not realized that the serving of tea to a guest in this country was as complex and ritualistic as the Japanese tea ceremony; it involved a great deal of sitting and waiting. There was a marvelous brazier to admire, which heated water in an even more marvelous copper kettle. A boy coaxed the fire along with repeated use of a bellows while Mornajay sat rather uncomfortably on a mat and watched. When the water was at last brought to a boil el-Kebaj arrived, to sit cross-legged on the matted floor with a tray holding glass cups in front of him, each filled with sprigs of green mint. This was accompanied by a bowl with great chunks of sugar. Water was poured into a cup and very gravely el-Kebaj added sugar and tasted it, his movements slow and sensuous. The tea was returned to the pot for added embellishments and the process began all over again.

Like wine-tasting, thought Mornajay crossly. He sat in a room with peeling cement walls decorated with the ubiquitous photograph of the King, and an Arabic calendar that advertised incense. There was a huge wood-and-glass buffet at the end of the room and one overstuffed European chair, otherwise the room was lined with rugs folded up in corners or unfurled on the floor. He suspected that he would be sleeping on one of them tonight, and this was when his optimism began to leave him as he wondered what the hell he could do for anyone who did reach Rouida, and what the hell he'd do if no one came at all? His time was limited here by his laissez-passer and he had to leave the next afternoon, unless by some means he could persuade el-Kebaj to approach the Prefect and win him an extension. It was true enough that he'd made contact with Khaddour Nasiri, and yes that was a triumph, or had been, and it was true that Nasiri had transport, but how on earth could any stranger wanted by the police arrive here to be spirited away without half the townspeople in pursuit?

The headman nodded at last, gestured to the boy who lifted the tray and carried the tea to Mornajay.

Mornajay forced himself to smile but it was difficult, he felt as if he'd cut the smile out of paper and pasted it on his face. "Merci beaucoup," he said, and hoped the glue didn't show.

19 • *It* would be a drive to remember, thought Mrs.

Pollifax, if she was to be allowed a future for remembering. She could discern no road or cart-track behind them as they careened ahead in the darkness over untilled ground. Placed in the rear of the truck, with nothing to grasp and hold on to, they were tossed around like marbles in a box, for although Rashid did not drive fast he drove with resolution, presumably following a known footpath. They bumped, they slithered and they slid, always on the slant as the truck mounted small hills, descended them and climbed again. Rashid drove without lights but the darkness was not absolute, he seemed to know where they were going but the only illumination came from the thin slice of moon high in the sky.

Now as the truck reached the top of a hill and swung briefly to the left she could look back and see the tiny village they'd left, only a cluster of tiny shapes now, but seeing it she clutched Sidi Tahar's arm and pointed. The lights of three vans, miniature now, were entering the dirt road by the cemetery and heading toward the village of Mahfoud and his neighbors. They had escaped just in time.

Sidi Tahar's gaze followed her pointed finger and he nodded. "Yes—Allah Akbar, God is great," he said simply, and then the truck swerved and they lost their glimpse of the village, entering a barren plateau of rocks.

On and on Rashid drove, until Mrs. Pollifax decided that hell was not a place of fire and demons but an endless drive in the night over rocks and stones toward an unknown and probably unpalatable destination. She had just begun to accept this new concept of eternity when the truck slowed and came to a stop in the shadow of two high pillars of stone. Max called out, "Are you all right?" A moment later his head appeared over the quarter-panel and he said, "If I'd known Rashid could drive this far into the hills I'd have had you sit up front. I'm sorry. I wanted to talk to him and I don't think even Rashid knew we'd make it this far."

Sidi Tahar said thoughtfully, "It offended the flesh, it is true, but not the bones."

"Oh it was *good*," cried Ahmad eagerly. "This is a *fine* truck!"

With dignity Mrs. Pollifax said, "I will climb out—if I can —but it would motivate the process to learn how many miles Rashid has driven us."

"Twelve or thirteen," Max told her, extending a hand to help her.

She did her arithmetic: from Zagora they had driven five miles to the house of Ahmad's aunt and uncle, and this truck had carried them twelve miles further; the numbers were not entirely satisfying but certainly they were an improvement, for they were now halfway to Rouida and Khaddour Nasiri. She watched Ahmad jump down from the truck; Sidi Tahar rose stiffly and was helped out; she herself gingerly climbed over the side panel and allowed herself to drop into Max's arms. She discovered that she could still stand upright and still walk, which she felt was a very real blessing, and a definite surprise to her as well. Once on solid ground again they stood and watched as Rashid maneuvered the truck between the two massive rocks; he backed it into the crevice with alarming abandon, turned off the engine and triumphantly saluted them. After an exchange of words with Max and Sidi Tahar he strode off in the direction from which they'd come; there was a long walk ahead of him but obviously it was made endurable by the thought of returning in a few weeks to claim and own the truck.

"He says we're well past the checkpoint on the road below us," explained Max. "We could take to the road but I think it's safer up here, don't you?"

"Unfortunately yes," she said, and looked down into the valley on their left that stretched for dark miles across a flat plain until it bumped into a line of mesas so uniformly flat they looked as if their tops had been sliced off by a sharp knife. Miles away she saw a solitary light shining in the great expanse of waste. It shone mysteriously, like a star. She turned and looked ahead of them, and in the moonlight saw a hill of rocks.

Noticing the expression on her face Max said reassuringly, "Rashid tells me that after another mile or two the hills slant down to meet the desert ahead—but unfortunately there are rocks."

"Yes," said Mrs. Pollifax, eying them with hostility.

"So let's go," said Max.

"*Bismallah,*" said Sidi Tahar.

"*Bismallah*," echoed Ahmad, beaming at them all.

And so they began their walk as the moon rose higher in the sky and the chill of night deepened, and for the first several miles it was like walking through a forest of stone. Strange surreal objects rose all around them, the variety of their shapes astonishing: rocks in phallic columns, rocks like enormous loaves of dark bread, and some—but this betrayed her growing hunger—like round flat pancakes. A few stood twenty feet high, with space just wide enough for them to squeeze between, others rose like walls that had to be circumnavigated, the smaller ones they climbed over on hands and knees.

Gradually the rocks grew less formidable, no longer walling them in, becoming lower in height, more accessible for climbing over. In the cold light of the moon Mrs. Pollifax thought they might even be following a path now that had been made by goat-herders or shepherds, or possibly—this thought was not kind—by other refugees from the law like themselves. It occurred to her as she followed along behind Ahmad that she didn't have the faintest idea what day of the week was about to dawn in a few hours, it felt an aeon since she'd left home and it came as a shock to realize that she'd not been in Morocco a week yet. She dismissed her confusion because she was too tired to count days and places on her fingers, which in any case were numb with cold. Vaguely she wondered where Cyrus was, and what he was doing—sleeping, probably—but it was kinder not to think of Cyrus or of sleep, either, or of how hungry she was and how cold.

Concentrating on Ahmad ahead of her, watching him manage the rocks with envied agility, she thought of the village they'd just left, and of how Mahfoud had talked as if Ahmad's father might never come to claim his son and she wondered again what he suspected and what he feared. His attitude had disturbed her at the time, hearing of it, and it disturbed her now. *We have saved a few lives,* she thought, *not many, not the life of Hamid ou Azu in Fez, and perhaps not the imprisoned Ibrahim in Er-Rachidia, but the young waiter in Erfoud was warned in time, and in Tinehir we saw Omar and his daughter safely off to the desert.* They had so far preserved Sidi Tahar's life and he had sworn to his silence concerning the informant ahead of them in Rouida so there was hope there . . . was it enough, what they'd done?

There was no answer to this because what had to be found now was a way to save themselves.

They had walked for nearly two hours when Max abruptly held up a hand to stop them. "Listen," he called sharply.

They halted, listening, and heard it too: the slow, steady drone of a machine tearing apart the silence of the night and moving toward them. "In the sky," Max said. "It sounds like a helicopter—at low altitude, too."

She said incredulously, "But surely they can't see us in the dark?"

"It's possible, yes. Oh God yes it's possible if they've night-vision goggles—and they'll have searchlights, too."

His words stunned her. "Hide!" gasped Mrs. Pollifax, and glancing frantically around her she pointed to a massive loaf-of-bread rock where erosion had carved away a hole at its base and left a shallow overhang. They raced toward it, rock-jumping to reach it in time, and crammed themselves into the narrow space just as the sound of the helicopter turned into a roar. She said with a shiver, "It must be *very* low."

The searchlight reached them first, an obscene and garish finger of light hunting for them among the rocks, probing, searching, almost human as it illuminated rock after rock—as if beating the bushes for game, thought Mrs. Pollifax, and the four of them the game it sought, to be flushed out and caught—while accompanying the light was the dreadful noise of this monster that hovered unseen above them. It was so near and so low that its blades whipped the air around them and stirred the tufts of grass growing in the niches of the rocks.

Both noise and light were terrifying; time stood still as they waited, listening, and she found herself holding her breath as if this would render them even more invisible, and then abruptly the monstrous machine moved on. Slowly the air and the grasses stilled, and the noise of the whirling blades diminished.

They had not been seen, not yet at least.

"They were after *us?*" asked Ahmad in a scared little voice.

Max said grimly, "Yes and they'll be back."

She didn't like the sound of his voice; she said quickly, firmly, "Yes but we have to keep walking, regardless. We have to reach Khaddour Nasiri and warn him."

"Unless he's already dead or in prison," said Max gloomily.

"Max," she said softly, "don't give out now, we need you."

He crawled out from under the rock and looked at her with exasperation. "You're bloody cheerful but you're right, of course, damn it. Okay let's go."

They left their refuge, moving more cautiously now, every sense alert, ears listening for sounds of pursuit, their eyes constantly searching among the rocks ahead for a new hiding place should they need it. It was half an hour before they heard the helicopter again, but this time it was in the distance. Taking cover they saw its searchlight pierce the sky some miles away: silhouetted briefly against the moon the machine looked like a macabre praying mantis with swollen belly and great wingspan. They watched it disappear, returning from where it had come, and left their hiding place to walk again.

Later, in the thin gray light between darkness and first dawn, they stopped to rest and to divide their one tin of sardines and the last of the oranges. They had not spoken for an hour or more. As she flung herself down exhausted on a patch of grass, her veil wildly askew, her cheeks flushed, Mrs. Pollifax gasped, "This certainly answers one question that troubled me."

"What?" asked Max, dropping down beside her.

She turned her head and grinned at him. " 'There's a dance in the old dame yet, toujours gai, toujours gai . . .' "

"What on earth!"

"A quote from *archy and mehitabel,*" she explained with a twinkle. "On the day that Carstairs' assistant called me about coming here—good heavens not even a week ago—I had just decided they must think me too old for any more assignments. I was brooding over this when the phone rang."

Max burst out laughing. "Thanks, I didn't think I could ever laugh again. You really thought that? You doubted?"

"Of course I doubted."

He looked her over in the dim light and shook his head. "I can't even remember how you looked when we met—very civilized, I'm sure. Now I'm traveling with this wild-looking peasant woman in a torn djellabah and cracked sandals, and as for myself I've been panting the last mile, and yet you really thought . . . I hope I'm not getting hysterical but I find that awfully funny."

She smiled at him sunnily. "Not that funny but do have some more orange. Sidi Tahar, how much further?"

He pointed ahead. "Dawn is soon and the rocks grow few. We are near the desert, the real desert." He said gravely, "You know, of course, the desert is where you must go now, it's the only way out of this country for you."

She realized that she'd known this for a good many hours but that it had been inadmissible to consciousness because of the overwhelming obstacles still between them and escape. She said with a tired attempt at humor, "And I've so carefully hung on to my return Casablanca–New York plane ticket . . . I even have my boarding card."

Max said indignantly, "You sound damned confident, Sidi Tahar, that we'll get to Rouida, find Khaddour Nasiri and get *out* of Rouida. How can you be so confident when you don't even know how to find the man? Is this your Allah again?"

"But I have visited the village a number of times over the years," he said calmly, surprising them. "I have enjoyed tea with the headman el-Kebaj and talked with him of the Koran—no, he is not one of us and he is to be avoided—and I have slept in Khaddour's house on my way to—" He smiled. "To other places."

"To the desert," she said, nodding. "To the Polisarios."

"Yes, where you must go now, too, before you can be delivered to Algeria for a new ticket and boarding pass."

But his words held no reality for her, they were blocked by too many uncertainties and a wall labelled Rouida, and so she relegated them to the country of dreams.

Max said impatiently, "But haven't you roused suspicions in Rouida, going there like that?"

Sidi Tahar shrugged. "I am invited here and there from time to time when it pleases Allah. I am known to wander, for it is a principle of the order to which I belong to help the poor, and the poor are everywhere." He smiled. "It is said that humility is the wealth of the poor, and that sitting with the rich hardens the heart . . . So says the law of the Brotherhood, built on the Koran."

"I see," said Mrs. Pollifax, touched by those words. Her glance dropping to Ahmad she saw that he was holding Sidi Tahar's hand now, and listening to him with an adoring look on his face. He was transferring his hero-worship to Sidi Tahar—which was for the best, she told herself sternly, because of the four of them it was Sidi Tahar who had the best chance of getting through to the Polisarios. She and Max were the outsiders, disguised Westerners and so *very* conspicuously sought by the police.

They buried the empty sardine tin and the orange peels in the gravel and started out again. "Not far, not far now," Sidi Tahar told them, and he took the lead with long confident strides, his djellabah flowing loosely behind him like a cape. The sky was lightening perceptibly in the east, the dark shadows cast by the rocks were shrinking and there was a freshness to the air, a suggestion of warmth to the cold night air, a stirring of wind. As they continued walking Mrs. Pollifax realized that she was walking on sand exclusively now and that they had left the rocks behind them. When a small hill rose up ahead of them Sidi Tahar held up a hand for them to stop.

"Listen," he said, smiling.

The early gentle breeze was delivering to them the sound of a rooster crowing. "A village?" she gasped.

"Yes, Rouida is off to our left. We will not climb the hill to see, we creep up the side of it, please."

It was a low hill, and crawling to its crest Mrs. Pollifax peered over the top and caught her breath because directly ahead lay the desert, that great lonely expanse of land uninterrupted by trees, villages and man, illuminated just now by the moon that was close to slipping away beyond the horizon. She looked and marvelled: here was the world of nomads and hermits, and of men of God like de Foucauld, of unseen oases and the graves of caravaners and explorers. She turned her head to the left and a mile away saw the shadowy outlines of Rouida, a cluster of low flat-roofed buildings hugging the earth.

Abruptly Max pointed and said, "Look! What's that?"

Far away on what had been an empty desert a moment ago a line of dark shapes was blurring the horizon, arriving there as suddenly as if they'd climbed a steep mountain to reach its crest and become visible all at once; the tiny figures stretched out in single line almost a mile from east to west.

"Those are camels, they have to be," said Max in awe. "It's a caravan!"

"So many," whispered Mrs. Pollifax and watched in amazement as perhaps a hundred or more camels plodded slowly out of the desert *hammada,* their very slowness speaking of long arduous days of travel, dust, endurance, heat. She said, "But I didn't realize caravans still existed. Sidi Tahar, what do they bring?"

"Many things," he said. "If they're unfreighted they would be camels on their way to market to be sold. If they're loaded they will be carrying trading goods from Mali and Senegal or Mauritania—spices, goatskins, copperware, ivory, gold—and also carpets and jewelry made by the desert nomads such as the Berbers and Tuareg." He shrugged. "For us this is good, it brings distraction. We will go down to Rouida before the caravan grows nearer—it is still an hour away—for when it arrives it will bring much excitement, and in that confusion—" He looked at them sternly now. "You hoped for rest, I know, but this is a gift to us. Come! Before it grows lighter . . . we must move like shadows and go."

Hearing him Mrs. Pollifax felt a stab of panic that sickened her. She wasn't ready to move on and it had nothing to do with physical stamina. It was her nerves that were raw and quivering now, she wasn't ready yet to learn whether this final attempt to escape would succeed or fail, the thought of more suspense was almost unendurable. She needed time after coming so far, she wanted to shriek her protest, remind Sidi Tahar that she'd not slept for over twenty-four hours, and she wanted—*needed*—to stay here in this coveted safety zone and rest. She wanted—

To take root here? inquired another part of her politely, *and for how long, Emily?*

It was, after all, a life and a future that Sidi Tahar was presenting to them; biting her lips she struggled to her feet.

As if he read her thoughts Sidi Tahar said gently, "It is all in the hands of Allah . . . it is written."

She nodded, remembering that, when translated, the word Islam meant submission to God and she wished that she had such faith, which to a fiercely individualistic Westerner seemed pure fatalism. From her childhood she wearily dredged up the expression that God helped those who helped themselves, and placing this next to Sidi Tahar's faith she found enough on which she might lean. Once on her feet she could even feel a certain giddy recklessness about what lay ahead. Perhaps something of the East had entered into her, after all, or perhaps she'd simply become too tired to worry. In any case, she thought, if she was found and arrested she would at least be allowed to *sleep*.

Sidi Tahar took full command now and gave stern instructions: Mrs. Pollifax was to keep her face veiled at all times, making sure only her eyes showed, and Ahmad was to walk beside her. If Max, with his stubble of beard, would keep his head lowered and shuffle his feet instead of striding along like a Westerner he would pass easily as a peasant from the hills, but he must be careful how he walked. He, Sidi Tahar, would do any necessary speaking because Max's Arabic was that of the cities and the people here were Berber.

Persuaded by his confidence they prepared to relinquish the protection of the hills, and in the dusk preceding sunrise they began their approach to Rouida from the west while the caravan of camels, still distant, approached it from the south. Mrs. Pollifax hoped they moved like shadows but as they left behind the last withered scrub she felt terribly exposed and vulnerable; there was nowhere to hide and they had been in hiding for so long that open space frightened her.

As they neared the village it emerged more clearly from the shadows, taking shape: she saw a circular well ahead, in what appeared to be an unpaved village square . . . and then she saw the car. It was parked not far away from the well, so out of place in this primitive scene that it added to her unease; it was an anomaly here at the edge of the desert, it didn't belong here, it implied a messenger from the city, it implied danger—but then, even worse, she noticed a man curled up asleep on the step to the well. Without hesitation Sidi Tahar led them past the man, who stirred, jerked awake and looked up at them with sleep-bleared eyes. *"Salam,"* murmured Sidi Tahar, and the man nodded, returned a reply but watched them with curiosity as they passed. She did not turn to look back but shuffled along behind Max, past a long building with a cola sign over it, and then Sidi Tahar mercifully drew them into a narrow alley between two buildings and she sighed with relief at reaching cover.

She said, "That car—"

Sidi Tahar nodded. "Yes, it had a Marrakech license plate. Watch your veil!"

She nodded, one hand clutching her veil tighter, her heart beating fast.

The illusion of cover proved short-lived, however, because the village was not asleep after all, its wakefulness had merely been hidden by its outer walls. In the passageway down which they walked the doors stood wide open to dark rooms with earth floors. There was the smell of cooking oil and of charcoal smoke; a barefoot child stood in a doorway and stared at them. Soon this passage intersected with another and they turned to the right, then to the left and right again, the streets bordered by continuous mud-stained walls broken only by doorways or tiny windows like eyes. *Dear God but this is a real maze,* she thought, and marvelled at Sidi Tahar's sureness. Twice they met the shadows of men huddled into their djellabahs, their sandals slapping the earth as they passed, and then abruptly Sidi Tahar turned and entered a long and much wider passage. At its farthest end Mrs. Pollifax saw light and space again—the desert —and realized that he had chosen this dark and crooked route to conceal them.

Halfway down this broad passage Sidi Tahar stopped at a closed wooden door and knocked lightly, rapidly. A voice called out from inside, and Sidi Tahar replied in his own language. A bolt was drawn and just before the door opened Sidi Tahar turned to them and smiled. "We are here," he told them. "We have reached the house of Khaddour Nasiri."

20. *The* door opened several inches and they were observed by a bright dark eye. "Praise be to God, you are here!" gasped a voice, the door swung open and in this manner they met Khaddour Nasiri, informant number seven. He looked a rough and burly man, with a heavy moustache and thick callused hands, but if he lacked the grace of Sidi Tahar Mrs. Pollifax was delighted at finding him safe, well and looking very competent. He gave Ahmad a startled glance, his eyes moved to Mrs. Pollifax's veiled face and then came to rest on Max. Pointing to him he said in English, "He is a *nasrani* but he has muscle, he is needed for my left tire!" and having said this he remembered the courtesies and bowed to Sidi Tahar, touching his hand to his forehead. *"Salam alaikum,"* he said.

Sidi Tahar smiled. *"Alaikum wa Salam."* He added quickly,

"I have come to tell you that everything is known, Khaddour, it is ended for us."

The man nodded. *"Bismallah,* I will be glad to go now—it is time, I have hungered and waited." He slipped into his own language, speaking quickly, with Max listening nearby.

Mrs. Pollifax glanced past him at the dark stone-walled room with its carpets and pillows, but not understanding what was said brought impatience, and she touched Max's arm. "What is it? What are they talking about?" she asked.

Max looked puzzled. "He seems to have somehow expected us, he has his truck ready to leave. Except for one tire."

She did not find this reassuring. "Sidi Tahar," she pleaded, "Max is saying we were *expected?"*

Sidi Tahar turned to her. "He tells me there has been someone here before we came, warning of trouble."

She gazed at him in horror. "Who could that be? Where is this person? Is it the police?"

"I know only that he has spent the night in the house of the headman el-Kebaj."

"But—" Agonies of anxiety arrived again. Khaddour regarded her with little interest and turned back to Max, speaking urgently in words foreign to her.

Max nodded and said, "There's no time for talk, he says a police spy came to the village last night and slept by the well. Right now he needs a strong helper for the left front tire, whatever that means. The important thing—but I'll try to learn more, except what does it matter?" He gestured helplessly. "We go or we're caught. You, Ahmad and Sidi Tahar are to wait here, he says not long."

Not long, she thought despairingly.

"Lock the door behind us," Max told them, and hurried out with Nasiri.

The door was locked and Mrs. Pollifax collapsed on a pile

of carpets and sat there hugging her knees. Ahmad sat down beside her, giving her an anxious glance, and Sidi Tahar, standing in the middle of the room, looked down at her thoughtfully. He said gravely, "Your spirit has become tired."

She nodded. "This is the last suspense of all, Sidi Tahar."

He shrugged. "But not the first."

"No—but we've tried so hard, and there is that car from Marrakech we saw, and the police spy who saw *us,* and the mysterious person who told Khaddour there was trouble . . ."

"The mind can hold only one thought at a time," he reminded her gently. "Think beyond Rouida, think of the Polisarios, in fact I will speak of them now, since as a woman you may appreciate their creed."

"Creed?"

"Why not? In which they renounce all forms of exploitation and affirm a fair distribution of resources, adequate house and health facilities, and free compulsory schooling—"

She glanced quickly at Ahmad.

"—and the emancipation of women," he added, "vowing to re-establish their political and social rights."

This was pleasing but still academic because those women were miles away across the border and she was here, and she was relieved when Sidi Tahar stopped talking. After a few minutes, still observing her, he said, "You remain stubbornly in your fears and worries, and not with us."

She had been thinking of Cyrus; she had been remembering the cool greenness of pine trees, of snow in the meadows, and warm hearth-fires, but his gentle accusation reproached her and she glanced up at him.   .

He said, "As a gift to you, to distract you—and for Ahmad, because he may become a Sufi, too, one day—I will do the dance for you." He shrugged off his djellabah, robed now in a long belted white shirt. He bowed, touching one hand to his forehead, and she thought his lips moved. He had captured her complete attention now. Humming a tune he began to sway, and then he stopped, took a firm stance, folded his arms across his chest and began to turn, slowly at first and then faster and faster until she gasped as his body blurred like a spinning top—he was like a flame—and she understood that this *was* his gift to her, and she came to life again, responding, so that as he slowed, becoming body and flesh again, there were tears in her eyes. "Oh yes," she whispered, "yes yes *yes.*"

Sidi Tahar's eyes glowed; he looked as if he returned from another world. "Of course yes," he said. "Always yes—to life, to Allah."

"And your left foot never moved," she said in awe. "Thank you, Sidi Tahar." And she smiled, feeling rooted again in the moment, and without fear.

Yet when the knock came at the door she jumped nevertheless. Ahmad raced to unbolt and open the door to Max, who ducked inside, closing it behind him. She saw that his face had turned haggard. He said in a low tense voice, "Quick—the place is suddenly swarming with police. The truck's waiting at the end of the alley—very exposed and—"

She said, "Dear God what's that noise, Max?"

"Camels," he told her, and with a flash of his old self added wryly, "Camels and police, it's insane. Sidi Tahar and Ahmad—you go first; Mrs. Pollifax and I will follow. We do it two at a time, but hurry—Khaddour's at the wheel, it's dangerous. Out and turn to your right and *run.*"

He opened the door to them and Sidi Tahar amazed her by the swiftness with which he made his exit, holding Ahmad by the hand. Max closed his eyes, counting "one . . . two . . . three . . ." He opened them and gave her a twisted smile. "Well, *Tante* Emily, it's our turn now—pray and run fast."

She nodded, he opened the door and they slipped through it to the alleyway. Turning to the right she saw the truck waiting for them some eight doors away in the sunshine, but as she broke into a run a voice behind them shouted, "Arretez! Halt!"

She looked over her shoulder and saw that two men in black leather jackets and visored caps had entered the passage and at sight of them had begun to run. "Police!" gasped Max. "Oh God."

Because they were so near, and because one of them was pulling a gun from his holster they had no choice but to stop. Beside her Max whispered, "Only two of them . . ." and with a quick glance, "Keep your face covered."

"They'd soon uncover it," she said in a low voice. "Take the one on the right, Max, I'll take the other." A hurried glance behind her to the truck showed her that Sidi Tahar was lifting Ahmad into its rear, but Khaddour could not afford to wait long. She turned to face the two policemen. Beyond them another man was just entering the alley and she recognized him —it was Saleh, last seen when he'd locked them into the storage hut in Zagora. *It's now or never,* she thought grimly, and as the two men caught up with them and began speaking harshly in Arabic she took a defensive stance and waited.

The taller of the policeman stretched out his arm to snatch away her veil with his hand, and this brought him near. With a quick slash she struck down his arm, aimed a kick at the nerve center in his thigh and when he staggered back in pain she drove the knuckles of her right hand into his jaw. Leaving him barely conscious on the ground she turned to Max and saw that he'd managed to wrestle the gun from the second man and was just hitting him over the head with it.

"Run!" she gasped, and punctuating her urgency a bullet ricocheted off the walls nearby; Saleh was armed and in pursuit, shouting for help.

They ran. There was no time to open the door of the cab, they flung themselves into the back of the truck with the others. Khaddour gunned the engine and turned the truck into the great broad avenue of sand that led toward the desert, threading his way among a dozen camels, huge and homely figures making ungodly groaning noises as their veiled and blue-robed Tuareg drivers unloaded them. Peering over the panel in the back Mrs. Pollifax watched Saleh emerge from the alley shouting, his lips forming the words *Stop them,* and because no one heard him over the braying of the camels he fired his gun into the air. "Stop them! *Regardez!*" he screamed, gesturing wildly.

The truck was moving with terrifying slowness; up ahead in the cab she saw Khaddour leaning over the stick-shift, his right arm struggling to push it out of low gear. They were leaving the camels behind but so slowly that Saleh, running after them and waving his gun, was ominously gaining ground on them. He had been joined by one of the camel-drivers—a Tuareg, she saw from his veiled face and indigo robes—and behind them other policeman were converging to join in the hunt. *We're not going to make it,* she thought grimly, *oh these trucks, these trucks, God help us . . . faster, Khaddour, faster!*

The slowness of their progress in low gear was agonizing, they had not even reached the last walls of the village, beyond which lay the longed-for desert. She felt Ahmad's hand reach for hers and she grasped it, sharing his fear. A bullet from Saleh's gun struck the side of the truck with a metallic *ping,* the camels brayed in the distance, the truck's motor roared senselessly, the shift remained stuck in low gear.

There was no hope, no hope at all, she thought in despair as Saleh and his companion outdistanced the others and drew near. *Please, Khaddour, please make the gears work,* she prayed, and as she hung over the back-panel of the truck to watch she saw the veiled Tuareg bring a gun from the folds of his robe and fall back a step to fire it.

"Down, Ahmad!" she screamed, and shrank lower. The Tuareg pulled the trigger and fired, but peering over the side of the truck she saw to her astonishment that he had not fired his gun at them but at Saleh.

She gasped as Saleh crumpled and dropped to the ground. The man in the indigo-blue robe and veil spun around to flee but in that moment of turning, before he raced toward the sanctuary of the walls, his veil fell away and she saw his face and gasped.

Their pursuers came to a halt beside Saleh, staring down at him in bewilderment, and at that moment the gears meshed at last and the truck shifted into high gear. As their truck gained speed the man who had shot Saleh disappeared into one of the mazelike alleys, but just before he vanished into its shadows Mrs. Pollifax saw him ruthlessly fling off his robe and she glimpsed a blue windbreaker and dark slacks.

Beside her Max gasped, "Good God, that man saved our necks, did you see that?" With a glance at her face he said, "Hey, are you okay? You look as if you'd just seen a ghost."

Mrs. Pollifax sat back, puzzled and astonished and thoughtful. "I did," she said softly. "I did see a ghost." And as she fully grasped what she'd seen—and whom—and interpreted all that it meant, she began to smile, her smile broadened, and suddenly she threw back her head and laughed.

Max shouted at her crossly, "My God, woman, we're still thirty-five miles from the border, what in hell can you be laughing about?"

"A joke," she shouted back at him. "A wonderful joke! A pompous bore of a man I met a year ago, never dreaming or imagining he could be one of Carstairs' people, when all the time—"

She did not finish; she would tell Max later, when there was no need to shout. Instead she turned and looked back at the village of Rouida, grown small now as they left it behind in their race across the desert, and she thought, *Salam Alaikum, Mr. Mornajay . . . I hope you trusted God but tethered your camel first and will soon be safely away . . .*

No helicopters came to intercept them, no trucks followed, and presently Mrs. Pollifax slept a little with her head on Max's shoulder. When she opened her eyes it was to wonder how she could have dozed off during such a wild and jolting drive across the glazed sands. Above them the sky was still drenched in the gold and apricot colors of dawn—she had not slept for long after all—and when Khaddour noisily pounded on the horn, which sounded like the braying of the camels, she realized it was this that had wakened her. She sat up and said, "What on earth—?"

"Look!" shouted Max, pointing.

Leaning over the side-panel of the truck she looked ahead and saw a subtle change in the terrain of the desert, saw a series of low dunes, saw a few goats feeding on impoverished desert grass and behind them a pair of low tents, and then she saw the men: two of them in coarse khaki-colored djellabahs that melted into the khaki-brown of the desert around them, their heads snugly wrapped in turbans that hid their chins, and almost their eyes, and each wearing a submachine gun strapped to his back. As she looked in amazement one of the men waved a pair of binoculars and the other, in a fever of welcome, unloosed a pistol from his belt and fired it into the air.

The truck came to a shuddering halt and the men rushed forward to greet Sidi Tahar, to help him down and embrace him with joy.

"But—who are they?" she faltered.

"Our escort—Polisarios," Max said in an awed voice. "They're telling Sidi Tahar they got his message and have been waiting a long time for him. We're being thoroughly welcomed!"

Welcomed, she thought; what a pleasing word that was after being pursued the length of a country, always in hiding, always hungry, and with almost no time to sleep. Now they were being welcomed by two of the men with whom she would begin her long journey back to safety, and to Cyrus, and home.

But it was Sidi Tahar who had the last word—as usual, she thought with affection. This friend of Carstairs' stood straight and tall beside the truck, with a small and weary Ahmad at his side. Glancing up and meeting her gaze he smiled and spread out his hands in a gesture that encompassed the great lonely desert, the fading colors in the sky, and all the hazards of living. "You see?" he said to her. "It was written thus all the time."

About the Author

Dorothy Gilman has chronicled the adventures of Emily Pollifax in eight previous books. She is also the author of suspense novels featuring other heroines and has written short stories as well as a dozen young people's books. She has traveled to many of the countries she's written about, has raised medicinal herbs on a farm in Nova Scotia, lived in New Mexico, and is at present in Maine. Her last novel, *Incident at Badamyâ*, was set in Burma, her favorite of the many places she has visited.

Book Mark

The text of this book was set in the typeface Caslon by Berryville Graphics, Berryville, Virginia.

It was printed and bound by Berryville Graphics, Berryville, Virginia.

DESIGNED BY ELOISE